BLOOD OF THE MOON

BOOK 4: THE RUNESPELL SERIES

SARAH BUHRMAN

Black Rose Writing | Texas

ISBN: 978-1-68433-803-0
PUBLISHED BY BLACK ROSE WRITING
www.blackrosewriting.com

Printed in the United States of America
Suggested Retail Price (SRP) $18.95

Blood of the Moon is printed in Adobe Caslon Pro

*As a planet-friendly publisher, Black Rose Writing does its best to eliminate
unnecessary waste to reduce paper usage and energy costs, while never
compromising the reading experience. As a result, the final word count vs. page count
may not meet common expectations.

Editor – Diane Morrison

BLOOD OF THE MOON

CHAPTER 1

A pair of shrieking voices stabbed into my calm facade. I barely kept from flinching before a jostle on my left, then right, accompanied the girls running down the promenade. They dodged around a handful of people who smiled at their rambunctiousness.

"Ella! Maria! Slow down!"

I glanced at the woman beside me, my mother, who shook her head as the girls ignored her calls. My mom caught my gaze and smiled. "I'm so glad we did this, Nicola. You've been running yourself too hard lately."

I shrugged, not sure I wanted to talk about my issues. "Well, you and the girls deserved some time away from Indiana's back woods."

A handsome young server appeared at my mom's elbow holding a silvered tray with two orange-y red mimosas in fluted glasses. "Marylou Crandall? Your drinks."

Mom took the drinks and handed one to me. The icy glass only accentuated the chill in the air. It had been getting steadily cooler as the cruise ship moved north.

Mom took a big sip. "Mmm, yes. We all have needed a good get away for some time." She wandered over to the railing and looked out onto the gray waves of the Pacific. "But you, especially."

I sipped at the drink, grimacing at the acidic-tart orange and cranberry juices that formed the base. "I guess..."

Mom brushed a handful of her thick black hair away from her face and looked closely at me. "I'm not kidding, Nicola. Ever since that awful situation with that horrible man, you've been really tense, like you just can't relax." She sighed. "I understand it. I mean, when someone attacks you, it's almost easier than when they attack and hurt your family, your children."

1

I felt her hand on my back, rubbing along my spine through the sweater I'd worn over my blouse. I let myself lean into her touch, craving the assurance that only a mother could give. "I'm still going to therapy," I said. "Maria, too, though Ella seems to have worked through what had happened."

Mom drew her hand back. "You aren't crazy," she assured me. "You don't need some quack digging through your choices and your situation–"

"Gods, Mom!" I growled, resentful that she had tainted the moment. "I don't go to therapy because I'm crazy! You don't have to be completely nuts to get help. You can do it to keep from going over that edge, too, you know!"

She flinched back, turning to stare out over the water again. "Sorry. I just don't understand why you would need to see a shrink. You are doing just fine."

I turned to look at her. "Have you ever considered that I'm 'doing just fine' *because* I see a shrink? Or that me 'doing just fine' is actually just a really good act that I put on so you don't worry about me?" I stepped away as she reached her hand out to me again. "You don't know me, Mom, and you seem more invested in what you believe is true than you are in my actual well-being."

"Nicola!" she chided. "Keep your voice down!"

I rolled my eyes. "Someday, I hope you care about me more than you care about what a bunch of strangers think. I'll see you and the girls at supper."

I turned on my heel and stalked away, swaying with the roll of the ship on the heightening waves. I dropped off the barely touched mimosa at the bar on my way through and made my way down to the family suite I shared with the girls. My mother had a single tiny room just next door, but she'd been spending most of her time with us on deck or playing games at the table in our suite – two bedrooms and a common room.

The cruise had been a big extravagance for us. It wasn't that we didn't have the money. Ella's father had left us enough to be comfortable for at least another decade. But growing up with very little and stretching every dollar as an adult made for frugal habits that were hard to let go of.

Some people reacted to sudden money by spending it. I – the odd duck, as usual – had invested it in a trust so that we could only access a certain amount each month. It meant we were taken care of, more or less for life, but we still had a budget to watch.

I flopped down on the comfortable bed and pulled one of the too-soft pillows over, squishing it under my head. I stared out the window into the gray, cloudless sky and let my thoughts drift until they were non-existent.

• • •

"Mama! It's supper time!"

Ella's voice roused me just before a double jolt of bodies landing beside me on the mattress shook me out of my nap. I stretched and rolled over, grabbing at the girls to pull them into a hug.

"Snuggle pile!" Maria crowed.

Both girls were around halfway through their ninth year, with the solid bone structures of their respective Hispanic and mixed ancestry. Neither one was delicate or wispy, so when they full-body flopped on top of me, I couldn't help letting out a grunt at the impact.

"Oof! Ahh! I'm drowning!" I squawked as the two giggled and struggled to get more firmly on the pile that was me.

After a few minutes of laughing and some exchanged tickles, we relaxed into a heap of hugs.

"Did someone say supper?" I asked, slyly. Knowing the girls, they were hungry. With the two of them looking at hitting puberty and a couple of growth spurts in the next few years, they were always hungry.

"Yeah!" Ella shouted jumping up. She flopped herself backwards on the bed and flailed. "Supper time!"

Maria, slightly more reserved, grinned. "Grandma sent us to get you," she said. "Are we eating in the big dining room again?"

I nodded. "Yes, we are," I assured her. "We get to eat there for supper every single day we are on this ship."

Her rich brown eyes widened at my words. I forced a smile for her. When I met her, she'd been abandoned by her own mother in favor of a new baby born to the leader of the cult they were in.

I mentally corrected myself – that WE were in. I had joined the cult to find one of the Runespells, but I'd found myself falling into the same traps as the other women. It was only the smallest of reassurances that it had been due to the cult leader using the power of a Runespell on us.

Maria still had moments of questioning whether she had the right to be in certain places or to do fun things. I tried my best to give her as much freedom as I could while still maintaining the boundaries that kids required.

I reached over and tugged on her loose braid, then hefted myself off the bed and grabbed the girls each by the hand. "We better get there before all the good food is gone," I joked.

We headed out into the hall and found my mother pacing. She stopped when we appeared and seemed about to speak, but she hesitated. I smiled at her and let the girls run ahead.

We walked in silence for a moment, then I spoke. "I know you don't understand why I do it, Mom, but I do need you to trust that I know what I'm doing." I glanced at her out of the corner of my eye.

She chewed on her lip for a few steps and then nodded. "I do trust you," she admitted. "I guess I just need to let my own biases go and accept that it's not necessarily what I think it is."

I reached over and wrapped my arm around her shoulders, pulling her closer to my side. "That's all I can ask for, Mom. I love you."

Her arm slipped around my waist and she returned the side-hug. "I love you, too."

Shrieks sounded out in the hallway ahead of us and we exchanged glances.

"We had better wrangle those monsters in before we get to the dining room," I suggested.

CHAPTER 2

"But Mama..." Ella wailed.

Maria sulked next to her and my mother stood behind them, her arms crossed over her chest.

I put my hand over my eyes and sighed. "Look, girls, I'm sorry. I just can't right now."

Ella pouted. "You always say that. You never go swimming with us."

Maria frowned at me and they stomped away to find something else to do. I glanced at my mom.

"What is wrong, Nicola?" she said. "You used to love to swim, but you won't go with the girls. Not once. Even getting you to play games with us seems like such an imposition on your time."

I sighed. I wasn't about to go into my recently developed fear of water, particularly cold water. Not with the girls so close. I wiggled the remaining toes of my right foot in the warm wool socks I wore almost constantly.

Two toes gone, along with my love of swimming. I sighed again, wondering if I could get one of those things back. The thought of getting into the chilly water of the cruise ship while sailing along the Alaskan coastline in October - it was just too much, too fast.

I shook my head. "Maybe we can hang out in the hot tub..." I ventured.

Ella rolled her eyes then went back to setting up the board game. "Grandma, are you playing?"

My mom shot me a dirty look before heading over to the girls. "Of course I am."

I let my shoulders sag as I watched them for a moment, then I turned away and went to lay down. I seemed to do that a lot on this vacation, much to the dismay of my family.

I pulled out my phone and checked my social media for something interesting. Ames and Hound Dog seemed to be doing well, although they weren't available for chatting today. Kaitlyn was busy with a new position in DC, and Joseph was at a conference for media personnel.

I sighed again. The problem with distancing oneself from people to protect yourself and them was that, eventually, you wanted to talk to someone, but they had already gone away. Boredom was the last stage of social dissociation.

I considered writing that down for Dr. Walters to analyze when we returned to Indiana. Instead, I rolled onto my stomach and let my thoughts wander yet again.

An alarm jerked me upright, and I blinked, rolling off the bed, confused. The lights were off, replaced by deep red emergency lights. Mom and the girls rushed into the room.

"What the he-heck?" I stuttered.

A voice sounded over the loudspeaker in the hallway. "Attention! Attention! This is a storm warning. Please remain in your rooms and secure all valuables. Staff will be making rounds to ensure you are safe and comfortable while we ride out this storm. Attention! Attention! This is a storm warning. Please remain in your rooms..."

The message repeated itself twice then there was silence.

I clapped my hands together. "Okay! Talk about an adventure!" I said with false enthusiasm. "It's a good thing we weren't swimming, huh? Let's get breakable stuff put down into drawers and things, then we can get back to the board games."

Maria grabbed my arm as the ship lurched. Ella launched herself at me and wrapped her arms around my waist.

"Shh. It's okay, girls," I assured them. "It's just a storm, right? A little wind, a little waves. This is a big ship, and it's made to handle these things."

"Are you sure?" Maria asked in a hoarse voice.

I nodded. "It would take an act of the gods to make this situation really dangerous."

Realizing what I'd said, I winced, hoping none of the gods had decided to take my words as a challenge. I peered out the window as the girls packed away toys and knickknacks to keep them from sliding off the furniture onto the floor.

After several hours of the ship being tossed around on waves that got bigger and bigger, and many more announcements about the state of the ship and the storm, we all piled up onto my bed where the rocking of the waves seemed less intense. The girls finally snoozed in my arms, exhausted by the tension. My mom watched the lightning out the window with growing fear, and I watched everyone with a firm knot of anxiety in the pit of my stomach.

A shudder ran through the ship, nearly throwing us from the bed. My mom and I clutched at the girls, barely keeping us all on the bed. After a moment, the ship seemed to stabilize.

"Nicola," she said, breaking the silence forced on us by the muted roar of the storm outside.

"Yeah, Mom?"

"I'm sorry I was so hard on you. I'm worried for you, and I don't know what's going on with you anymore."

I sighed. "That makes two of us, Mom."

She opened her mouth to speak again, but a pounding on the door interrupted. She slipped off the bed and staggered across the lurching floor to answer it. I could hear the shrill but professional voice coming from the hallway.

"We are evacuating the ship! Please exit the room and put on your life jackets, then follow this man to your assigned lifeboat! Do you understand these instructions?"

I shook the girls awake and moved to the door, dragging them along by the hand. I glimpsed the woman who had spoken as she moved on to the next room. It occurred to me there were only a handful of reasons to be making the announcement door-to-door, and none of them boded well.

A frightened-looking crewman stood waiting for us, holding an armful of life vests. Another family stood silently nearby, waiting to be led away by the same man.

I swallowed my panic and grabbed the life vests, handing one to my mom and helping Ella and Maria into theirs, carefully securing the closures. I slipped my own vest over my arms as I herded the girls out into the hallway. I nodded to the crewman and worked on my own vest closures as we walked quickly up to the deck. I had to remain calm for the girls' sake.

A third family joined us as we lurched up a short flight of steps and out onto the deck. I was promptly hit in the face with a spray of icy water as waves crashed into the sides of the cruise ship. The crewman directed us with barely audible shouts and exaggerated gestures to grab ahold of the ropes strung along the sides of the ship.

I wedged the girls in between my arms and held on with both hands, craning my neck around to be able to see the crewman. Mom grabbed on as well, keeping an eye on the girls. They both had fear in their eyes, but they quickly grabbed the rope and held on with their small hands.

The crewman spoke with another sailor and then staggered back over to us and the other families. "Time to get on the lifeboat," he shouted over the wind and crashing waves.

I blinked another splash of water out of my eyes and frowned at him. "Why are we abandoning the cruise ship?" I demanded. "Those little boats can't be safer–"

The man glanced at the other adults who stared at him, waiting to hear his response. "Did you ever see the Titanic?" he said, finally. "What happened when it sank?"

I swallowed, ready to laugh off the joke, but the man's grim expression told me it wasn't an attempt at humor. The cruise ship was going down and we had to get off of it. The scene where the Titanic sank and literally dragged people down with it flashed through my mind, but I pushed it away.

I blinked again, not sure if it was sea water or tears this time. The lump in my throat and fear lodged in my gut didn't help clear that up. I nodded to the man and we moved along the flimsy rope the other sailor had strung up from where we clung to the side of the ship to the lifeboat.

He helped the first family get into the boat, then the girls and Mom were next. Before I could get my feet on the steps, the ship lurched and I fell to the deck. One of the kids of the family behind me, a young boy of maybe five years, tumbled several yards away. The mother shrieked, reaching after him, but too afraid to let go of the rope.

I glanced at her husband, who held her and their other child tightly, and the crewmen, who were busy keeping others on their feet and safe.

"Shit!" I yelled into the wind, and I marine-crawled towards the child as he wailed.

I barely reached him, hooking a couple fingers around a loop on his life vest, when a huge wave crashed over the deck. I felt the cold water all around me and I fought the urge to scream.

A hard object banged into my legs, and despite my panic, I wrapped my legs around it, locking my ankles together. The wave receded and I found myself wedged in the railing of the deck with my calves locked around one of the supports. My numb fingers were entangled with the nylon cord of a life vest, and the child in it flailed his arms as he dangled halfway over the edge.

I grabbed his arm as it moved past my face and pulled him back up on the deck, rolling as best as I could. I unwrapped the cord from my fingers and rewrapped it around my right hand, then marine-crawled on my left side to the wall of the ship.

I grabbed hold of the rope and pulled us both up, hefting the boy and yelling at him to hold on. His arms squeezed my neck, but I ignored it to hold the rope with both hands. We made our way back to the lifeboat, shivering in wave- and rain-soaked clothing.

A bare yard from the boat, the rope ended, having pulled loose in one section. I looked across the space, frustrated. With the waves, it was too much of a risk to try to walk across the heaving deck without something to anchor us. The crewman stared at me, seeing the problem and obviously equally frustrated that he could not help us.

The frustration and anger seeped into my mind, and I felt the familiar tingle as yellow washed over my vision. I nodded to myself and looked over at the crewman. One good jump, I thought.

I held the boy with one arm, gripping the rope with my other hand. I let myself feel the roll of the ship on the waves, waiting for my cat instincts to take over.

Then I jumped.

CHAPTER 3

I crashed into the startled crewman, shoving the boy into his arms. Then my shoes lost all traction on the wet deck and my feet skidded out from under me.

Somehow, my hand slipped out of the nylon cording of the boy's life vest, which kept me from pulling him away with me. I was thankful for that, at least, as I scrabbled my hands and feet along the slippery polished wood. The heaving deck and gravity pulled me away from the lifeboat at an angle toward the ship's railing. Screams from the people on the lifeboat followed me as I slid away.

My hand hit a hard object and I slapped my palms at it, wrapping my fingers around one of the rail posts. I took several deep breaths and prepared to make my way back to the lifeboat for the third time. The sound of the storm was suddenly muted, and I stared in numb shock as a giant wave crashed down on top of me.

• • •

I didn't remember drowning before, at least not consciously. Experiencing it again was both strange and familiar. The cold had already been working its way through my arms and legs when I went overboard, and the total submersion finished numbing them into uselessness.

The waves pushed me under the surface, tumbling my body over and over, pulling me down like ropes tangled around my body. When those waves ripped the haphazardly fastened life vest from my torso, it was almost a relief, slipping under the buffeting waves into the calm depths of the ocean.

Then I was floating, semi-conscious and fighting the urge to breath in. Shapes moved in the water, just out of sight, shadows of waves rippling at the edges of my vision. I could see the faces of the Hands of Asclepius as they pushed me down under the freezing cold water. Their eyes were empty, dead, as I soon would be.

Something jostled against my numbed leg, causing my whole body to wobble in the mini-currents of icy water. I blinked. Surely it was too cold for sharks in this water. I looked around but could see nothing in the dim, greenish haze. The brief surge of adrenaline abated when nothing came of my fears, and I was floating, sinking, once more.

I thought about Ella and Maria. My eyes burned and I wanted to weep, knowing I would never see them again. I wouldn't be able to make it up to them, not going swimming when they'd asked. I would never be at the bottom of their snuggle piles. I would not hear their laughter or see their smiles. I wouldn't watch them grow into strong young women with minds of their own and hearts strengthened by their trials.

I tried to picture them as adults. Ella, with her deft touch and quick mind, would be an asset to any corporation, but she would really shine if she started and ran her own business. Maria, kind of heart and loving all creatures, would be a wonderful biologist or veterinarian. I tried to picture them tall and mature, hanging out with friends or eating at restaurants with their partners.

But I couldn't see their faces, not as adults. They wore power suits and pencil skirts in my mind, but their faces were still the faces of my children.

A shapeless form skimmed overtop of me, brushing against my hair and sending it billowing into my face. I tried to move, to brush it away, but my arms wouldn't cooperate, and then the water was still and calm around me once more.

I still fought the urge to breathe, the urge to cry, and I wanted my mother. I wanted my mommy and I wanted her arms around me, comforting and protecting me, the same way I comforted and protected my girls. The same way I had held the little boy as we made our way back to the lifeboat.

I hoped my mom was safe, and the girls, and the little boy and his family. I hoped they at least didn't need me anymore in this disaster. And, maybe, with me gone, the troubles would stop. Maybe the curse of my hero-for-the-gods status would bypass them with me floating under the waves.

I could feel the chain with the Runespells around my neck, nearly weightless in the water, yet dragging around my throat like a stone. The burden of that choice had not been sitting well with me, but I felt a little sad about not finishing what I'd started.

I frowned as the chain got heavier, as if reacting to my thoughts. The pendants, the Runespells, weighing me down, pulling me under, dragging me to the sea floor. I shook my head, certain it was in my mind, but I could see the vague shapes of seaweed and rocks moving just under my useless legs.

I was moving and moving fast. I looked down and around, searching for any clue as to what was happening. Then I saw it.

A tentacle was wrapped around my left ankle, pulling me along. And the size and shape of the appendage indicated something... huge.

I was dragged through a clump of seaweed and found myself at the edge of a drop-off on the seafloor. The shifting shape of a creature writhed in the crevasse, glowing with the light of a thousand bioluminescent organisms.

It was much like a giant squid, only no squid was that size or had a mouth that opened with a toothy beak like that. The creature dragged me down to it and, with the last air in my body, I screamed.

• • • •

I coughed and gasped against the rough, pitted surface of wet rock under my cheek. Water gushed out of my mouth and I choked on the gag that it triggered in the back of my throat.

I shifted, weakly trying to lift myself up as my abdomen heaved. My empty stomach cramped with the effort. Thin bitter streams of bile pushed up my throat into my mouth. I struggled to calm my body's reactions. Tears leaked from my eyes at the pain and helplessness.

Finally, the heaving stopped. I laid on the grainy rock, shivering and panting. After an eternity of reaching for stability within my body, my mind began to stutter into conscious thought again. I blinked and scowled, flashes of memory skittering behind my eyes.

The storm. The boy. Falling overboard. Drifting under water. The–

"Gods!" I pushed up and immediately felt dizzy. Black fuzziness filled my head, pushing out the memory of the... What had it been?

I barely managed to stay in a half-sitting position as my head cleared. The numb black fuzz was replaced with a piercing ache, driving spikes into my temples and down my spine.

I concentrated on breathing. If I started crying, the headache would only get worse. In and out. In and out. I coughed, hacking up the last drops of water in my lungs, and then winced.

"Oh dear gods, that hurt," I muttered.

My eyes fluttered open after a moment and I saw a bronze goblet near my right shoulder. It was held by a large, muscled hand, though that didn't bother me at all. A smooth, amber liquid sloshed inside the cup, and the scent of cinnamon and honey hit my nose, making my stomach rumble with craving.

I took up the goblet and sipped as the hand – definitely masculine, I noted – retreated behind me. The liquid slid down my throat, soothing despite the mild tinge of alcohol. It was room temperature, but it felt warm in my gut compared to the cold of the cave.

I realized there was no entrance in the rock's face, and I glanced down at the water. Memories of the creature returned. I sipped the mead and considered my situation a moment longer before rolling onto my knees and turning around before sitting back down with a heavy sigh.

The man before me was at least three feet taller than I was, built like a gym rat. He had long greenish blond waves of hair that fell past his shoulders, merging with a thick beard that covered his chest.

All in all, he was more attractive than not, but he was also very much not human. His eyes glinted gray with a green sheen to them. He wore only short breeches, tattered into rags below the knees. His calves and bare feet, as well as his upper arms, were covered in a silvery-gold sheen of what seemed to be scales.

I reached up to the chain around my neck and grasped the pendants dangling there. One burned with energy as I drew on it, seeking the knowledge of all the gods and god-creatures.

" Ægir," I whispered. I swallowed hard and bowed my head briefly, forcing my voice to cooperate. "I thank you for the drink. You are renowned for your hospitality and your ale. Both are well earned."

The jötun perched on a rocky outcrop and leaned his muscular arms on his knees. "Then it is true," he rumbled in a voice like waves crashing on a rocky shore. "The Aesir have recruited a hero to act on their behalf."

I stared for a moment into his intense gaze, feeling warmth steal through my body. I blinked and glanced down at the rocky floor in front of me. I wasn't inclined to giving in to physical attraction or desire, but the draw of Ægir was that of a warm sea in summer – cool, refreshing, soothing, enveloping.

I cleared my throat. "Uh, yeah." I snuck a glance up at him, then dropped my eyes again.

The sea giant leaned back, and I could feel his eyes on me. If this was Ægir, then he was married, and his wife wasn't someone I would want to think I was trying to step on her wifely toes. Most Norse gods had what could only be described as open relationships, but that would be quite an assumption to stake my life on.

"I need you," he rumbled.

I jumped at the words, confused by what he said in the context of what I'd been thinking. "W-what?"

He laughed. "It would be more appropriate to say my wife needs you," he amended. "However, she tends to be less... um, diplomatic. So I am opening the conversation on her behalf."

I glanced around the cave. I didn't see any sign of the giantess. Nor could I determine the source of the light that seemed to infuse the entire cave. I sighed. Gods.

"Ok," I said. "Maybe you could give me a little more detail before I commit. I don't like to break my word over something as simple as making promises I don't know I can possibly keep."

"Ran is finishing up putting Cranky back to bed," he murmured.

"Cranky?"

The sea god grinned. "My little nickname for her favorite pet," he said. "The Kraken."

He turned his face to the water to my left. Out of the corner of my eye, I saw the water roiling as if it had been left on the boil too long.

"My love," Ægir called. "Our guest is ready for you. But please, don't kill her before you get your information."

My head jerked from the chaotic splashing to his face. He smiled at me reassuringly as a blue-green skinned woman nearly as tall as he rose from the sea.

CHAPTER 4

The woman placed a lovely foot on the rock. Her blue-green seaweed gown, streaked with red and rust seaweed accents, drifted down over her ankles. She had black hair that was pulled back into a messy, thick braid. Her slender face seemed just a little too sharp to be human, with her nose and chin ending in delicate, narrow points. Her eyes were the dark deep blue gray of the ocean depths, like her husband's.

She reached out a hand, her bones too delicate for the sheer, proportional size of her body. The effect should have been gawky or anorexic, but she managed to appear liquid and lean, more serpentine than awkward.

Ægir reached forward and took her hand, guiding her back to where he'd perched on the rocks. I noticed there were two indents where the giants could recline against the surface.

The sea goddess greeted her husband, then turned to watch me as she settled against the rough stone. Her eyes were inhuman, devoid of compassion. It reminded me of the Norns. I swallowed and clutched the Runespells, knowing none of them would be able to help me so far under the surface of the water.

"You are she who holds the Runespells, then?" Rán spoke, her voice fluid and echoing oddly. I thought it was the underwater cave that caused the echo, but I quickly realized her voice naturally echoed like an underwater cave. It created a double reverberation that sent shivers down my spine.

"Well, mostly," I said, my voice cracking. I cleared my throat, hoping she would attribute the break as a physical effect of nearly drowning, not as a result of the fear she inspired.

"Mostly?" Her black brow rose against the sea-blue of her forehead. "Either you are or you aren't."

I shook my head to clear it. "I am collecting the Runespells," I said. "I don't have them all. I can't say I hold the Runespells because I only have some of them. But I also can't say I don't because I do hold some."

Ran's mouth tightened. "Is that so?"

I swallowed again and nodded. "Yeah."

The blue-green giantess leaned forward, a movement that might have been sensual if she had been human. Instead, it was simply intimidating. She stared into my face. As much as I wanted - needed - to look away, I couldn't tear my eyes away from those haunting depths.

Ægir reached over and laid a gentle hand on his wife's arm. "Beloved," he rumbled. "Allow me..."

Ran sat back, a small frown on her face. Her eyes never left mine, but I was able to blink and look away. I turned my gaze to Ægir.

"My dearest wife is the goddess of sea storms," he said. "It is her power and her right to cause the oceans to rise up in fierce anger and destroy those who dare to sail our waters. She has always held her power in moderation, seeking only to keep those who traverse our waves in the fear and awe that we deserve."

I frowned. "Well, that's one way of looking at it, I suppose." I felt a surge of anger that these jötun wanted to hurt people just to intimidate them.

Ægir smiled, as if reading my thoughts. "You don't approve. Tell me, then. How do you humans treat nature when you do not fear and respect it properly?"

I scowled. "We... well, I guess we abuse it."

Ægir nodded. "You have abused it. And, now, only the fear of super storms makes you think twice about continuing to abuse it. Only the destructive forces of what you have wrought keeps you even the smallest bit in check."

I sighed. He was right. Climate change was a non-starter for people and corporations, at least until the idea of Category 5 hurricanes and "snowmageddon" came into play. It was a frustrating thing that, too often, respect for the rest of the world had to be imposed with the threat of destruction of resources and those oh-so-precious material goods that the material, capitalist societies held dear.

"Fine," I conceded. "Sometimes you have to use the stick instead of the carrot on us."

Ægir smirked. "Only sometimes," he offered dryly.

"What does that have to do with me?"

"Someone is calming my storms," Rán snapped. "Someone is using the Runespell to undermine my power, my authority."

I blinked and thought back through the Runespells. "The Ninth Runespell?"

The giantess nodded sharply. "My ability to keep human effects on the world in check is being held at bay. My duty to protect the balance of the world by inhibiting mankind's unthinking actions is being stolen from me. And I want to know if you are the one trying to muzzle me!"

I recoiled at her anger. "Me?" I squawked. "No! I don't have the Ninth Runespell. Not yet."

Ægir patted his wife's hand, calming her by degrees. Then he turned back to me.

"You do not have this Runespell?"

I shook my head. "No, I don't. I give you my word."

He nodded and turned to watch his wife. She bit her lip in frustration and glared at me.

"It is nearby," she said, finally. "I can sense it close. It is being used against me somewhere in this area."

I took a deep breath and hefted myself to my feet, hoping I wasn't about to do something I'd regret. Technically, it was what I'd signed up for, and I was pretty sure I would end up regretting it after all was said and done. I shook off the dread that fell over me and took another deep breath. "Then, I offer you my services."

The jötun couple exchanged a glance and looked at me blankly.

"I will search out the Runespell," I promised. "I will get it from whoever is abusing its power and keep it safe from others. You will then have free rein to act as you see fit to keep mankind in check."

Ran sneered. "That is a fine start," she said. "However, this slight cannot be borne. I will have my vengeance, as well. I want the wielder of the Runespell at my feet."

I swallowed. "I-I can't promise that," I admitted. "If it's a child who doesn't know better, or-"

"There is no excuse for this!" Rán raged. The water behind me roiled up again with her fury.

I shook my head. "If it is a person who deserves to be punished for it, I will gladly turn them over to you." I lifted my eyes to meet those terrible blue-gray depths, steeling myself against the fear they invoked. "That is the best I can do. To do otherwise would violate my own morals, my own Orlog."

The jötun were visibly taken aback by my words. They watched me closely for a long moment.

Ægir finally nodded once. "We cannot demand that you violate your moral boundaries."

Ran pursed her lips. "Very well. I will give you until the next blooded moon to make this right."

"Blooded moon?"

"The full moon, when it drips red with blood, warns those who love and respect me that I will take lives should they venture out onto the water. That sign will tell you when my patience has been stretched too far, so do not delay."

The giantess gestured for me to step forward. It took a long moment before I could convince my feet to move. She reached for the chain at my neck, and I flinched but held my ground.

"This crystal will summon me," she said. "You have only to touch it and will me to come to you, and I will know you have found the person responsible and that you choose to turn them over to me."

I frowned as something ice-cold dropped against my breastbone next to the Runespell pendants on the chain. I considered her words and nodded. After all, if I chose not to summon the sea goddess, I didn't have to.

"It is time for you to return to the upper world," Ægir murmured.

A roaring noise grew behind me. I spun around as the water leaped up, roiling over the rock ledge and covering me to the knee before I could grasp what was happening. I bit back a protest and took several quick deep breaths before hauling in as much air as I could. The water lifted my feet from the rock and swirled past my neck, then over my head.

CHAPTER 5

I slowly released the air in my lungs, hoping to avoid the bends but afraid of running out of the precious oxygen. I kept my eyes squeezed shut, feeling the water pulling and tugging at my clothes and limbs. Even if I could see which way to go, I wouldn't be able to fight against the water. I could only hope the jötun wanted my services more than they wanted some petty vengeance against one random human.

I could feel the air running out, and I stopped letting it bubble out, hoping what was left would hold me over until I breached the surface. The force of the water seemed to lessen with each passing moment. I lost track of the minutes, focusing on holding my breath against the fear chattering at my ankles and the draw of the sea's own innate peaceful seduction.

I finally opened my eyes, peering into the blue-gray depths so much like Rán's gaze. I couldn't make out anything of use and I felt my body sag against the water, hopelessness filling me. After all that had happened, both today and years ago, despair was not an unexpected reaction.

Some objective part of my mind knew the feelings were not helpful, and that I was still alive, so there was hope. But emotions are not objective or logical. Even knowing that Ægir was likely speeding me to the surface didn't keep my eyes from burning with tears that instantly mixed with the cold sea water. I struggled against the urge to sob, working to keep my anguish from literally killing me.

A loud rushing noise caught my attention and I blinked twice before my head thrust above the waves. I gasped in a reflexive breath before gravity pulled me back under the water. I kicked my cold-numbed legs and reached for the surface with lethargic arms.

It seemed too long before I broke the surface again. This time, I kept myself bobbing along the surface of rough waves. I gasped for breaths between saltwater slapping into my face.

It took several moments for me to stabilize myself enough to look farther than the next wave coming at me. I finally spotted a dark shape rising over the waves, but I couldn't tell what it was. I struggled towards it, mostly for lack of any better destination.

Twice I stopped, trying to float on my back for a few moments of rest. It helped only a little. I was able to relax my cramping muscles, but the lack of constant movement left my fingers and toes numb in the cold water.

That more than anything else got me moving again. I was terrified that the seductively numbing cold would rob me of more than a few toes this time. The cycle of resting, fear and struggling against the waves went on forever before the exhaustion threw the balance off, and I simply floated, staring into the gray sky.

My eyelids drooped and I felt a distant terror at what would happen if - when - I passed out. A burning in my eyes told me that tears were trying to fall again, but I was simply too worn out to cry.

I felt something jostle my legs. My whole body jerked, and I sank down before I regained the delicate balance of floating. I frowned, thinking it would be ridiculous to drown over a particularly rough wave-

Something bumped my arm, and it was definitely not just a wave. I gasped and thrashed in the water, moving from a back float to treading water. I jerked my gaze around, searching for a sign of what could have touched me. My panic dumped a fresh load of adrenaline into my system, giving me the energy that had escaped me just moments ago.

I whirled around to check the waves behind me for signs of sharks or, more likely, orcas thinking I was a seal. Either one would likely consider me a nice snack.

My skin became hypersensitive with fear, and every splash and wave sent ripples of fear through me. A particularly firm wave nudged me between the shoulders and my arms and legs moved before I could even process it, spinning me in the water to look behind me.

I screamed into the face of a puppy.

Puppy? No, that wasn't right. What had a doggy face and whiskers in the ocean, though?

I stared at the face until the word "seal" made its way through my brain fog. I began to relax. Seals weren't terribly dangerous, as sea creatures went.

As my mind cleared more, I considered the implications of staring down a seal while freezing to death where the Gulf of Alaska met the Bering Sea.

"Land!" I meant it to be an exclamation, but it came out a hoarse whisper barely audible to my own ears over the waves.

Seals lived on land. That meant there must be land somewhere... within the hunting range of an animal that could swim much farther than a human.

While I was focused on my thoughts, the doggy face of the seal had vanished. I sighed, hoping that the presence of the seal at least meant I was going the right way. But there was no way for me to know that.

I heaved a breath and began swimming again, thankful that the shock of the seal's touch had given me a second - or was it third or fourth? - wind. My legs kicked weakly, but I was moving.

After a few moments, I paused, trying to catch my breath. I was so exhausted. I couldn't tell what was numb from the cold and what was just completely worn out on my own body. I wanted to sleep so much, almost as much as I wanted to cry in self-pity.

I reached for the cat, my own inner Berserker energy, but there was nothing to fight. This was about endurance, not strength or agility. Yes, it was a survival thing, but not in the same way that triggered the Berserker.

I gritted my teeth and forced my hands to reach out in the half-hearted swimming strokes I'd been using. One hand hit the water and pushed under, cupping to pull as much as my strength could manage. The other hand pulled up and reached, slapping the water and going under.

I felt something under my palm. The slight shock wasn't enough to give me any more boosts. Instead, I tried to place the texture - a wiry, almost fluffy cover for something quite firm. The object moved under my hand and the puppy faced seal popped up again.

Without thinking, I reached out and grasped the creature midway between the head and where the flippers came out from the body. Before I could process the situation more, the seal began swimming, and I struggled to find the undulating rhythm that would allow me to breath as the mammal dragged me through the waves.

I almost didn't know what it meant when my foot hit something in the water. The seal shook itself out of my grasp and vanished. I struggled to tread water, working to comprehend something, anything.

My foot hit something solid again. It happened a half-dozen times before my brain caught up. By that time, I was only a few yards out from a gravel-filled shoreline. I slipped several times trying to get my feet under me as the waves got stronger so close to the shore.

I nearly cried with how long it took me to scramble onto the beach and out of the waves. I considered just falling face-first onto the rock-filled beach, but I couldn't ignore the likelihood of hurting myself even more that way.

Instead, I staggered across the beach until I found a smooth spot near the sparse tree line. The trees were mostly firs, and there was a carpet of needles that buffered what rocks still poked out of the ground as I laid down as carefully as I could manage - which meant I tried to catch myself as I fell down.

I let my head fall back, adjusting the angle of my neck to find the most comfortable spot. I was shivering violently in the cold wind, with my clothes still soaked with sea water and clinging to my skin. I panted for several minutes, hoping to find the energy to get up once I was more rested.

Instead, I felt the heavy cotton of exhaustion filling my ears. I fought drifting off half-heartedly. As my vision darkened, I taunted myself that I could hope so strongly to be saved that I could almost hear human voices in the sounds of wind, waves and squawking sea birds.

•   •   •

I felt warm. I nearly cried at the dry heat against my salt- and wind-chapped face. I wriggled ten fingers, eight toes, delighted at how they tingled in the heat.

"She's moving."

"That's a good sign. Leave her a bit longer."

I shifted my head vaguely in the direction of the feminine voices. I wondered who it was, but the thought didn't stick around long enough to pursue.

I thought about opening my eyes, but they were shut so nicely. I told my eyelids, quite sternly, to lift, but they were too heavy for even the firmest order to budge them.

I turned my attention to my mouth and vocal cords, sure I could make conversation until my eyes cooperated. A bare rasp of a whisper hissed in my throat. My mouth stayed as firmly closed as my eyes.

Well, this wasn't very polite of me. Here I was, toasty and pleasantly alive, and I couldn't even be a good host.

My mouth twinged, the corners flicking downward briefly.

Host? That would mean I was at home. But the smells, the sounds - these weren't familiar to me. This wasn't my home.

I considered this information carefully. I sniffed the air more carefully. There was definitely a wild, salty, fishy smell to the air. Not unpleasant, but not the smell of my landlocked, forest-bracketed home, often filled with the smells of broth-based soups and fruit and nut pastries that I helped the girls learn to cook.

The girls. My mouth twitched downward again. Where were my daughters?

I jerked, feeling my arms spasm under a rough woven blanket. This time, I managed a full groan.

The second voice spoke again. "Fetch some broth."

My legs jerked, the muscles twitching violently when I tried to move them. My eyelids, finally obeying my previous commands, fluttered. I caught a vague glimpse of a dim, cluttered room.

An arm pressed under my shoulders, lifting me into a slightly sitting position. I could feel something being shifted behind my back, then I was lowered back against several pillows.

I struggled to open my eyes again, but they only fluttered in a rapid blink that gave me little to see.

"Shh. Here, sip on this. Careful, it's hot."

The first voice I'd heard murmured in my ear. I turned my head slowly and let the lip of a mug push my lips apart. Hot broth - not chicken or beef, maybe fish? - scalded my mouth, but the taste on my tongue short-circuited any reaction to the temperature. I gulped at the liquid as fast as the voice would let it pour down my throat.

"Okay, that's enough for a moment."

I whimpered in protest, then another cup touched my lips. I gulped down the cool water, and it soothed the mild burns on my mouth and tongue from the broth.

"There you are. You just take it easy for a little while longer. You are safe here. Grandmama and I will make sure you get better."

I slumped back into the pillows and drifted off to the sound of the voices reassuring me.

CHAPTER 6

My eyes fluttered open at the sound of someone moving around nearby. For a brief second, I thought it might be one of the girls, and I opened my mouth to ask what they were doing.

Instead, my eyes focused on a young woman who looked like she might still be in high school. She had the round face and heavy lids of Asian peoples, and her dark, straight hair matched that. But I'd been near the shoreline of Alaska when-

The memory of the cruise ship going down hit me, followed by the surreal encounter that had followed.

The young woman rushed to my side as I lunged upright, then gasped at the effort when my abdominal muscles collectively cramped.

"Please, be still. You are still very dehydrated and will have trouble moving until your body gets back to a healthy balance."

I blinked up at her. She was the first voice. The one who had reassured me. The one who, with her grandmama, had brought me back from the edge of death.

I flinched away from the thought that that particular edge was becoming quite familiar.

"Would you like water? Broth?" she asked.

I nodded as vigorously as I could manage. She brought two mugs and handed me the cold one first. I drained it quickly, then the taste caught up to me.

"Vinegar?" I croaked.

The young woman nodded. "And sugar. Just a touch of each to help give you electrolytes while you hydrate."

She handed over the warm mug and took the empty cup from my hands. I sipped at that one, my thirst temporarily eased by the odd vinegar drink. The broth warmed my gut and filled my belly in an oddly satisfying way.

"Who are you?" I asked, then blushed at the brash way it had come out. "Er, I mean..."

"It's okay," the woman said. "People recovering from near drowning usually find their filters are water-logged."

I grinned at that.

"My name is Cora," she said. "This is me and my grandmama's home. She is Mary Kusugak, elder of the tribal council. Welcome to Storm Bay."

I blinked. "Storm Bay?"

Cora nodded. "We are southeast of the Kodiak islands. It's a small village, a small island, but we do well enough."

"Island?" I sat up again. "Oh, no."

Cora frowned. "Hey, we may be Yup'ik but we have all you will need to recover, and we will get you to the mainland as soon as possible. We have already sent a boat to get help."

"Help? Is there something wrong with me?" I eyed the blanket and fought the panicky urge to check my limbs.

"No," Cora assured me. "We just don't have the resources for all the survivors."

"Survivors?"

"The shipwreck? The cruise ship?" Cora shot me a confused look. "Isn't that how you ended up in the ocean?"

I blinked. "Uh, yeah. I just thought I'd ended up far from everyone else." I gasped as a thought struck. "Is my family here, then? Mom, my girls?"

Cora smiled. "Maybe. What are their names? I'll see what I can find out."

I gave her the names and she left. She seemed to be gone forever. With the knowledge that there were shipwreck survivors on the island, all of my fears about my family's safety came crashing back. Despite my attempts at staying calm, my limbs were icy and my breath came in pants by the time the door crashed open again.

"Mama!"

The twin voices called out and my head whipped around towards the sound. My eyes went wide, then my vision blurred as tears filled them.

"Ella! Maria! You're safe!" I held my arms out and was rewarded with the double crash of their small but sturdy bodies against me. My arms tightened around them and I squeezed, reassuring myself that they were real, warm and alive.

"Nicola!" My mother's voice came a bare moment later. "Praise God, you made it!"

I lifted my eyes to hers and reached out a hand for her to take. Her cool, dry palm was a comfort against my fingers. I pulled her closer and, after a moment's hesitation, she wrapped her arms around the whole bundle of me and the girls.

I let my eyes drift closed and sighed. I couldn't imagine anything better in this moment than my family close and breathing and not in danger.

•   •   •

"The storm was horrible," Mom said, stroking my hair and Ella's in turn. Maria was tucked in on the other side of me. With a daughter under each arm, there was no room left on the narrow bed, so Mom had pulled up a wooden ladder-back chair.

I swallowed against the lump in my throat as she continued. "We nearly capsized several times before we reached the shore here. We didn't even have time to think about what had become of you until the people here helped us drag the boats onto the beach. Then we had to take head counts and figure out what to do."

"We thought you was lost at sea," Ella piped up.

Maria nodded solemnly, her huge eyes glued to my face. I smiled reassuringly at both of them.

"I'm fine," I said. "Just a little swim, right?" I met my mother's eyes over Ella's head. "What happened to the boy?"

"Caleb," Mom offered. "He and his family were in the same lifeboat that we were. They were fine, if overwhelmed. They kept—"

She stopped and pressed her lips together a moment before she cleared her throat and continued. "They kept thanking me for what you did. I think they felt guilty that you might have... not made it."

"Well, now we can give them the good news," I said, forcing a bright note into my voice.

"Actually, they aren't here anymore."

I frowned. "Where—?"

"About half of the survivors went on the supply boat," Mom explained. "We wouldn't all fit, but the villagers wanted as many of us as possible to get back to the mainland, so we wouldn't strain their resources too much."

Cora spoke up from where she was stirring a pot in the small kitchen area a few feet away. The house was essentially a large room with a private bathroom and two small bedrooms. The bed I was on doubled as a couch and guest bed in the tiny space. "We didn't want any of you to not be provided for, and we knew we wouldn't be able to care for all of you for long enough for the boat to make a round trip."

Mom nodded at her words. "They should be back in two or three weeks, depending on the weather. They will let the local coast guard know what happened, though the coast guard may get here sooner, just because of the sunken cruise ship."

"It depends on if they think to look here," Cora pointed out. "They tend to overlook us."

I grimaced at the sardonic note in her voice. "I can imagine. So the flare has been sent up, and now we are just waiting here with a group of generous islanders?"

Cora raised an eyebrow. "Well, we aren't exactly isolated," she pointed out. "We actually have a research station on the other side of the island, and another group of visitors who set up a camp about a hundred yards from the eastern side of the village."

I tried to hide my surprise and failed when my eyebrows rose. "Oh, uh. Cool. What kind of visitors?"

I felt my mother's cool hand on my arm. It was a psychologically restraining touch, which set the hairs on my nape on end.

"They are Christians, Nicola," Mom said, as if delivering terrible news.

Cora snorted, drawing both of our gazes. "Missionaries," she confirmed.

I shrugged my shoulders and grimaced. "I don't hate Christians, Mom," I muttered. "I hate people ruining other cultures just because they believe they are more right about something as subjective as religion."

"The Bible isn't subjective," she sniffed. "It is the written word-"

"It's redundant," Cora declared, interrupting the old argument.

I frowned. "The Bible?"

"No," Cora chuckled. "The attempts at conversion. The Yup'ik have been encountering Russian Orthodox, Moravian Protestants, and Jesuits for the last... oh, about 200 years. Almost all of us are primarily Christian, with only a few completely going back to our cultural roots for our spirituality."

"Oh," Mom said. "Then why are they here? Are they providing aid or something?"

Cora shook her head. "We are pretty self-sufficient. Not rich, mind you, but we do well. The US Government provides a little help when we do need it." She glanced up at us before returning her gaze to the fish stew she been working on. "They just don't think we are the right kind of Christian. Not that they ever ask what kind we are."

I caught the frown on my mother's face, but I couldn't help nodding in understanding. "Sounds about right," I said. I only hoped the snark in my voice hadn't been so obvious to Mom as it seemed to me. "So it's the Yup'ik, the missionaries, and shipwreck survivors."

"And the seal women," Cora interjected.

"The what?" I asked, my mind going back to the puppy-like face of the sea creature who'd essentially saved my life.

"Seal women," Cora said again. "It's a group of scientists – marine biologists – from Ireland. NUI Galway, I believe is the college. They study local fur seal populations from the research station. They don't interact much, but you might see them from time to time. They are actually the ones who found you on the beach." She jerked her chin in my direction.

"Well," I said, ruffling the girls' hair. "It's just a regular Grand Central Station here, isn't it?"

The girls laughed at my flippancy, but I couldn't shake the feeling that the convergence of so many disparate groups was less than coincidental. Considering my divine mission, I had to consider that Ægir had sent me up where I would end up in the one place where the Runespell was most likely to be found.

CHAPTER 7

I paused in the doorway and peered southward, towards the ocean waves. I usually wasn't quite so sure of my directions, but it was just after lunch and the sun was low in the sky in front of me, thanks to the late season and high latitude.

It was chilly – more brisk than really cold – and several people bustled around the streets. They weren't really in a hurry so much as they had purpose and direction in their walk. On the other hand, any time someone called out to another, they both stopped to speak, even if for only a moment. There were no dismissive waves of greeting that said the person waving had more important things to do than to talk to the other. The subtle difference in that interaction here versus what I usually saw in the lower forty-eight told me a surprising amount about the people.

I glanced down, just a little too wobbly yet to not know exactly where my feet where going. I stepped carefully down the two steps, even as Cora stepped up behind me. I glanced up at her with a sheepish smile. She had told me to wait for her to head out, but I was impatient.

Cora rolled her eyes and shut the door before putting a hand at my back, ready to help me if I should need it. Even the small touch was stabilizing as I walked carefully over the half mud, half gravel street that doubled as a sidewalk.

With a few murmured directions from Cora, I made it to the tiny community center where many of the remaining shipwreck survivors were camped out. Military cots lined the walls, stacked up for the day while tables and benches filled the center of the main room.

A few people were putting up about half of the tables to clear space for more energetic play, while others opened ancient board game boxes or shuffled a deck of cards for a handful of sharp-eyed elders who looked like they'd played more than a few rounds of gin rummy.

Kids ran around playing improvised games of tag on the open floor and 'the floor is lava' on remaining benches. Occasional squawks and screeches pierced the air.

I was immediately drawn to the small group that seemed to be forming at one table. There were a few people I recognized from the cruise ship, as well as some who were obviously native villagers. Two others seemed to be in charge of the group as an organized unit, though. They greeted the others and passed out small booklets filled with tiny text and basic drawings as illustrations.

I stood nearby for a moment, then my mother moved up to join the group. She had the girls and spoke to them briefly. The girls glanced at the younger kids running around and shook their heads, then the three of them joined the table, pulling up chairs.

I frowned. They hadn't even seen me. Of course, I hadn't really wanted to be noticed by them or by the group's leaders, but the fact that they hadn't seen me hurt. Deeply.

I moved up closer trying to catch what they were talking about. My gut told me I wasn't going to like it, and the first few words from the leaders confirmed that.

"Today, we will look at the story of Jonah," the woman missionary said. "How many of you have heard this story?"

There was a show of hands and I put up my hand as well. The woman's eyes suddenly shifted to me. They widened slightly, as if she was surprised to see me, but then she gestured for me to pull up a chair. I did, right next to my mother, and accepted one of the booklets.

"What are you doing?" Mom hissed.

"I could ask you the same thing," I muttered, looking at Ella and Maria meaningfully. "You don't get to decide their spiritual education."

Mom pressed her lips together, then, almost as if the words were against her will, she spoke. "Someone has to watch out for their souls."

The woman missionary spoke again, pushing a strand of brown hair behind her ear as she did. "Sometimes, God sends storms into our lives. Here, we see the storms of the sea even as we stay safe on land. Safe, at least, until the storm blows over us."

The man next to her nodded. "God said, 'Go to Nineveh, that great city, and speak out against it; I am aware of how wicked its people are.' He told Jonah to leave his home..."

I tried to listen to the words and ignore my mother. I wasn't up for having yet another fight with her about how I raised the girls. It was just so constantly draining as a single parent to have the one person I was supposed to be able to rely on for support and advice telling me I was wrong because we had different beliefs.

"And Jonah told the sailors to throw him overboard," the woman said. "Can you imagine the faith he had to believe that his sacrifice would save others? Faith only because of God's words in his ear. Words that no one else could hear."

"Many people would just dismiss such communion," the man took up the narrative. "It's crazy, right?"

I sat back and snorted. My action drew the missionaries' attention.

"You think he was crazy?" the woman asked me.

I could tell by her body language that she had expected – or hoped for? – someone to have my reaction. I smiled wickedly, knowing my response would not be what she expected.

"Nope," I said. "I do the same thing."

The woman's eyebrows rose. "You hear God's voice, then?"

I shrugged. "Only if I visit him in his garden. And we don't get along much these days. It's the others that I look to for what needs to be done. Although, it's usually the ravens that give me the really helpful information."

"Ravens?" the man said, confusion written all over his face. "What ravens?"

"Odin's ravens," I clarified. "They are just messengers, but they have great senses of humor." I paused thoughtfully. "The valkyrie don't joke around much, though Rade did make that one funny comment. Usually, the gods don't talk much unless they really need me. Well, these days. Before, they were happy to give insight and support, but now that I've been tapped, they are more demanding."

"Gods...?"

"Yeah," I nodded sagely. "Odin was first, but Tyr is my favorite, I think. The Norns are hella scary, and Hel is just plain inhuman. Most recently, though, it was Ægir and Rán."

"Rán?" the woman frowned. "Is that a...god?"

"Goddess," I clarified. "Well, jötun, which is like a god, but less human-like. They are sometimes called giants, and they tend towards more primal and elemental ideas instead of what we might call civilized concepts. But then, sea storms are pretty primal."

The missionaries exchanged glances. "God sends the storms as warnings and punishments," the woman began.

I snorted again, interrupting her. "Tell that to the woman I met a few days ago, just after being dragged across the bottom of the sea by the kraken."

"The kraken—?" the man choked out.

I nodded. "Cranky the kraken," I added with a grin. "At least according to Ægir. He's Rán's hubby. Much more approachable than she is, let me tell you. But then, he wasn't the one demanding a sacrifice."

"Sacrifice?" the woman gasped. "You think it is appropriate to make sacrifices to pagan gods?"

I smiled at her, staring into her eyes. "You mean, ask someone who has angered and betrayed a god to throw themselves into the sea to prevent harm to an entire... oh, say, a ship full of people by way of a violent oceanic storm?" I paused, letting the parallels to their own lesson sink in. "Not sure I think that's something I have the right to pass judgment on. The gods, even your god, ask people to do things for their own reasons. We don't always get to know what they are."

Mom pushed her chair back and stood up. "If you'll excuse me," she said to the missionaries, shooting a meaningful look at me. "I think I'll skip the rest for today. Girls?"

Ella and Maria stood up looking somewhat confused. They glanced at me, but I waved them off to join their grandmother before turning back to the missionaries. The rest of the group was glaring at me or muttering among themselves, but I ignored them.

"You," I said, pointing at the missionaries, "have some nerve acting like your version of religion is the only one that is valid enough to have communication with deity or 'signs' like storms." I glanced around. "Any relationship with any deity can include that. But dismissing it because it isn't yours, with your god, is hypocritical crap and a level of elitism that your own god's son warned against."

I walked away with as much dignity as I could manage, though I still felt weak and shaky. Cora appeared just as I reached the center's doors.

"Ready to head back?" she asked. "I didn't think you'd want to be up too long."

I smiled at her, pushing my anger back. She didn't deserve it, after all. "Yeah. I would like to have my daughters come by later today."

Cora nodded. "We'll get you settled, then I'll see if I can find them."

I nodded back, grateful that someone, at least, wouldn't be making me fight for every need and feeling I was having in my recovery. I rolled my shoulders, wondering if there was some additional trauma I should be considering.

For a moment, I wished I were home where I could just pick up the phone and give my therapist a call. Part of me cringed at being so dependent, but I remembered the alternative - beating in Zaro's face in my own backyard, double-tapping Bob in the cave. Now, I just needed to throw some poor soul into the jaws of whatever "pet" Rán chose.

I was beginning to think I wasn't meant to have a relaxing vacation.

CHAPTER 8

I slumped back against the pillows as the girls left. The visit had been awkward, more awkward than I'd hoped. They were confused as to why I was upset about them joining the bible study group, which meant they thought I was upset with them.

I'd tried to reassure them that I was upset with my mother for making it a thing, and with the missionaries for doing... well, what missionaries do. I figured I was more upset about losing control of things I felt should have been in my control. It was an uncomfortable emotion that usually resulted in me lashing out.

So the girl's visit was stiff and lacking the comfort and surety of emotional balance. Because of that, when my mom cut the visit short with a half-hearted excuse after only an hour, I didn't protest.

After another few minutes, alone with my thoughts, the door opened again. Mary, Cora's grandmother, slowly climbed the steps into the tiny home. I smiled at her, genuinely happy to see the woman who had been so generous towards me.

"Nicola," she said. "Did you get out today? Sea air is the best healing salve of all, you know."

I nodded. "I did," I assured her. "Cora helped me get over to the community center."

Cora appeared at Mary's side as the older woman sat in the old, sturdy rocking chair. She covered her grandmother with a quilt and handed her a steaming mug and moved the woman's crochet basket closer.

After passing another mug to me, she spoke. "Nicola doesn't care much for the missionaries, Grandmama."

My eyebrows rose in surprise. I hadn't realized Cora had seen what happened at the bible study. The young woman was more perceptive than I'd given her credit for. "I don't care much for anyone willing to run roughshod over people's culture and beliefs to get their quota for conversion."

Mary smiled softly. "It can be amusing watching those with less... situational awareness try to impose themselves on others," she offered. "We are used to it here. We've had missionaries almost on a constant basis for centuries. I think dealing with them and balancing their agenda against our own needs is our culture now."

I shook my head. "It's a shame."

"Would it be such if it had been another native tribe, five hundred years ago?" Mary asked.

I frowned. "I-I don't know. Probably not."

"The result to us is the same," she pointed out. "The only change is how you perceive the ethical, the philosophical, aspects."

I nodded slowly. "I hadn't considered that," I admitted.

Mary tsked as she finished her tea and set the mug aside. She reached down to pick up a ball of dark multicolored wool yarn. She plucked the crochet hook out of the ball and smoothed out the line of stitches that had already been made.

"You look at things from the qat'sqaq culture's perspective. There, the ethics is important. The whiteness of the invading culture is key. You are still centered on you. To us, the culture that is being choked out by an invasive kelp, such things are only academic." She peered owlishly at the line of stitches, then began moving the needle so fast I could barely keep track of the hook's location in the bundle of yarn.

I gaped as the line of stitches became a round cuff, then began to grow into something more. I stared in fascination for a long moment, then glanced down at the now chilled tea in my hands. I gulped it down and eyed the magic of the elder's craft again. I was pretty certain a mitten or glove was emerging from the cuff like ice crystals spreading across a window.

"It still shouldn't be allowed to happen unchecked," I said, finally. "Such an imbalance may have absorbed cultures in the past—"

"Like Rome," Cora called from the kitchen. I could see her working at an old laptop at the tiny kitchen table.

"Yeah," I said. "I guess. Rome conquered cultures and required they join the empire, which ostensibly let them keep most of their traditions."

Cora snorted. "When you are allowed to keep stuff just 'cause it fits with the other culture, that's not really much of a concession. Those restrictions were more socially imposed than legally, so it hardly counted."

I nodded. "True, but that doesn't justify it happening now."

"Ok, but it is their subculture to invade and convert," she said. "Stopping them is forcing them to change their culture. How do you do this so it is not passing judgment on one culture over another?"

I frowned for a moment, then shrugged. "Sometimes we have to pass judgment and live with that choice."

Mary chuckled. "All well and good, but someone is going to think it's unfair. Sometimes, that someone will be you."

I sighed. She was right and I knew it. I didn't like it, but that was the same thing that I'd had arguments with Joseph about in the forests of the northeast. He'd tried to use my sense of morality to appeal to me. But it hadn't worked. Now Mary and Cora were arguing the same, and they were using the very doubts intrinsic to the problem to make their point.

"You're right," I said. "So what do you do? What do I do?"

Mary chuckled. "I crochet. You rest. The Yup'ik adapt into the new culture or die. The missionaries... they keep saving souls. At least, that's what they think. But there will always be a part of us they cannot claim. Not for their god. Not for their culture. Though that piece may die from atrophy someday, they cannot have it."

I blew out my cheeks and let my eyes slide shut. It was a lot to take in, and I was still running too close to empty to keep up.

* * *

Cora led me to a door at the back of the main room of the community center. I'd asked if they had a library, since that had been my hope when we'd come the previous day. She nodded to another young woman, an older teen who I'd seen at the bible study the other day.

"Nicola, this is Elizabeth. She runs the library."

I shot Cora a look, hoping she wouldn't leave, but she made her excuses. "I promised Catherine I would give her a hand with supper prep today. I'll meet you in a half an hour to take you back, but I have to get meat pulled out of the freezers or I'll be behind schedule."

I turned back to Elizabeth. "Um, hey."

The teen had the same round Asian-ish features as the rest of the villagers. Her dark brown eyes looked me up and down and she gave me a tight-lipped smile. "So, you have a white savior complex?"

I blinked. "Excuse me?"

She shrugged. "Just wondering why you'd make waves with the missionaries. These ones are pretty nice, so we aren't really wanting them chased off by some atheist with a vendetta."

She turned to unlock the door, then stepped inside and held the door open for me.

I stepped through. "I'm not an atheist, and I don't have a vendetta, I just don't understand why your people feel the way they do—"

I stopped and stared behind the teen. The room was a small office or a large storage closet. Someone had built rough shelves into the walls, going from floor to ceiling. Each shelf was weighed down with dozens of books. Two small freestanding tables filled the center of the room. One held a laptop with what seemed like dozens of wires coming out of it, while the other had a ledger for signing out books.

She followed my gaze. "What? Did you think the Yup'ik were illiterate, qat'sqaq?"

I frowned at the word: white one. After Mary had used it, I'd asked Cora what it meant. "I'm not exactly white, you know."

She shrugged. "It is a cultural adjective, not a descriptor of melanin."

Her explanation was an impressive combination of social and political awareness. I nodded acceptance and turned back to the books she had stacked up. She had a wide variety of classics, texts on philosophy and history.

I tapped the spine of Mein Kampf and shot her a look. She shrugged. "Know thine enemy."

I grinned and went back to looking through the titles. I quickly realized that about half of the books were young adult dystopian. I gestured to the shelves filled with tales of chosen ones and girls falling for vampires. "You all like some light reading about basic white girls?" I joked.

Elizabeth glanced at them. "Nah, those are research."

I raised an eyebrow at her.

She rolled her eyes. "You think dystopia only happens when there is some big, single event. Plague, war, alien invasion. But that's just because you are part of the central city."

I gave her a questioning look. "Central city?"

"You are qat'sqaq, one of the Wives of Gilead," she said. "You are a Citizen of Panem. You are the Inner Party in Oceana. You, qat'sqaq, live in Rome. Because of that, you have your *panem et circenses*, cheap food and reality TV. You don't have to think about how your food comes so cheap or who is hurt for your entertainment. Some of you do anyways, but you don't have to."

I shrugged uncomfortably. "I'm aware of my privilege."

Elizabeth shook her head. "You literally can walk away from this. It isn't your life or death on the line. But we live in the lands of the resources, not the consumers. We have to seriously think about whether our survival can co-exist with the survival of our traditions and culture."

I swallowed. "But—"

The girl shook her head. "You come here, qat'sqaq, and you try to help us against the missionaries who want our souls. That sounds good, but many of my people think that our souls are the price we will have to pay to not watch each other die."

She paused pressing her lips together. "Then you say we can have the traditions of our people and the benefits of modern America. Don't you think we have considered that? You offer compromise as if we couldn't think of it."

I opened my mouth to protest, but she cut me off again. "Maybe you haven't specifically said that yet, but others like you have. You insult our intelligence because you think you are more worldly. But you do not understand our history. You offer compromise as if our people haven't been compromising since the first qat'sqaq came here."

I stared at her, not sure what to say.

She watched me with impassive eyes, then spoke again. "Which book would you like to check out?"

CHAPTER 9

"Ah, Cora, thank you. Mary, good to see you."

Cora held the door open as a woman who looked to be in her 50s climbed up the steps with a great deal more energy than I expected. She smiled at the younger woman than turned to Mary who gestured to a ladder backed chair that had been placed near her only a second ago.

"Catherine," Mary greeted. "Come in. Have some tea!"

"Is it that delicious fruity blend you like to hoard?" Catherine whispered with conspiratorial glee as she plopped down on the chair.

Mary nodded. "Oh, yes. Cora dear?"

Cora grinned, already on her way to the kitchen and the electric kettle that perched on the corner of the counter. She'd told me they had finally gotten it only because Mary could go through a half dozen or more cups of tea each day without even blinking. The kettle heated water faster and without taking up a cooking surface.

Catherine glanced at me. I tried not to spend all of my time watching Cora, Mary and their frequent visitors, but the only alternative I had while still being mostly bed-bound was the two books I'd gotten from the library. Still, I tried to keep my gaze modestly averted.

"I'd heard you'd found a drowned fish," Catherine said. "Perhaps you could introduce me to the gal who survived the winter's worst storm without a life vest or lifeboat? Such a miracle!"

Mary smiled. "This is my guest, Nicola. She did indeed survive such a storm in such conditions." She winked at me. "Though she was also, indeed, a drowned fish by the end. Nicola, this is Catherine Tudlik, daughter of the previous mayor, granddaughter of the last great alignalghi, and, though she will deny it, alignalghi herself."

Catherine pished and accepted the steaming mug from Cora. She turned and saluted me with it. "Greetings, Nicola."

I nodded solemnly and murmured, "Nice to meet you." I hesitated. "What is ah-li-gah-nal-gee?" I stumbled over the phlegmy, guttural pronunciations of the "g" sounds.

Cora laughed in the kitchen, while Mary and Catherine grinned.

"Close enough, qat'sqaq," Mary chortled.

Cora brought me a steaming mug of tea as well. She winked as she handed it over. "Don't let grandmama fool you. Most qat'sqaq wouldn't have done half as well and she knows it."

Catherine nodded. "Alignalghi is what you would call shaman or medicine man. Or woman. But it is too much honor to give this fumbling old lady such an ancient title." She held up a hand when Mary made a sound of protest. "The old ways have been lost to us. Even I know only a little of the great knowledge of the sea and the spirits that live in wind and wave. I don't speak for the spirits to our people, nor speak for our people to them."

I listened intently, intrigued and eager to learn about the Yup'ik spirituality. "What kinds of spirits? What would you say to them?"

"The spirits are those of the animals we hunt, of nature and the seasons," Catherine explained. "We thank the spirits of the whale and the seal for their lives. We thank the fish. And we invite them to come and take what they need in compensation."

I frowned. "What kinds of things do they take?"

The shaman shrugged. "We sometimes leave out gifts, and you can tell when the spirits take too much because people get sad and angry. Once in a while, someone will get sick when the spirits decide they want one of us to join them in the Skyland or the Underworld."

I blanched. "That's... wow."

Cora smiled as she pulled up a chair near Catherine and handed Mary a new skein of yarn when she fumbled. "It's a little more brutal than you are used to, eh, qat'sqaq?"

I nodded. "I guess," I admitted. "Though I doubt things were as nice and shiny as many historians present them. Even the Norse were known to be pretty hardcore in their acceptance of the perils of nature." I thought about Rán and Ægir. "In fact, the sea gods were considered primal forces who intentionally drowned sailors, and it was believed you should carry a piece of gold to placate Rán lest your afterlife be less than pleasant."

Catherine pursed her lips, considering. "The sea can be quite aggressive. The spirits are not malicious, per se, but they also have a larger balance to protect than the value of human lives."

I sighed. "Tell me about it." I sipped at the cooling tea. "I'd like to hear more about those who can talk to spirits, though. If you don't mind, that is."

Catherine smiled. "Some believe they could calm certain aspects of the wind and waves by their ability to negotiate with the spirits. The ability to calm a storm was rare but much loved in a shaman."

"Really?"

Catherine shook her head and smiled. "It was likely that any weather control was only the result of guessing and hoping," she assured me. "We don't seem to have enough ability to control the weather to keep our village safe from the rising waves, even."

I frowned. "What do you mean?"

Cora jumped in again. "Climate change," she said. "The oceans are rising and our lands are not high enough or large enough to hold back the waves. We are going to have to abandon our village and our island in only a few years."

"That's why the missionaries are here," Mary said.

"To help you move?" I asked, feeling like I was missing something.

Cora laughed. "To make sure we are properly Christianized and 'civilized' before we have to move to the mainland."

I frowned. "That's... not necessary."

Catherine waved her hand dismissively. "It is only to help us fit in with those on the mainland," she insisted. "We will be attending their schools, celebrating their holiday traditions. The more we are like them, the easier it will be for our children."

Cora snorted. "That may have been the case decades ago, but diversity is more accepted now. We could keep our traditions."

Mary frowned into her mug and handed the empty vessel over to Cora. "Be a dear and fill me back up."

Cora rolled her eyes and stood, taking the mug to the kitchen. Mary and Catherine exchanged a look that I couldn't read, then Catherine stood as well.

"Mary, a lovely visit as always," she said. "But I must be heading back. I have another meeting in about half an hour, and some people always have to be early."

Mary chuckled and the two women hugged briefly. Catherine turned to nod at me and then left almost as energetically as she had come in. Cora huffed her breath as she brought Mary her freshened cup of tea.

I laid back against my pillows, sensing the tension in the air. Something was underlying the conversation, but I couldn't tell what it was, or who was hiding things. I blew out my cheeks and wiggled my toes. I knew I was getting much better by the way I was getting restless more often.

Cora noticed my fretting. "How about we go to the community center again tomorrow," she suggested.

I nodded, glad for any reason to get up and move about. "Should be a blast."

CHAPTER 10

Cora didn't bother holding my arm or even hovering close by while I walked down the muddy path. The sky was gray and the light low. The sun was far too close to the horizon compared to what I was used to, even in Indiana, and the dim light weighed on my emotions.

"How do you combat the seasonal blues?" I asked Cora.

Cora shrugged. "We don't get it as much as you would think. Our diet is high in fish, especially salmon and herring. Those are both really good sources of vitamin D."

I nodded. "So you don't usually get the vitamin deficiencies that cause seasonal depression."

"It happens," Cora admitted. "Grandmama would say it's the salmon spirits taking back too much from us."

Her tone said she preferred the more scientific explanation, and I chuckled along with her at the perhaps overly spiritual reasoning her grandmother favored. We reached the community center after a few more minutes of comfortable silence. There were a lot more people milling around than I'd seen there before, much more than just the shipwreck survivors and a handful of the native people to help out.

It seemed the missionaries had come into the village in force. There were at least a dozen men and women in plain, cheap suits, long skirts, and very slick hairstyles. There were also many more of the villagers than I had seen in the center at any one time.

I turned to Cora. "Is there something going on?"

Cora shrugged. "Let's find out."

She led me over to a group of younger adults and spoke softly to them. I hung back, trying to not be invasive. After a moment she moved back beside me and heaved a sigh.

"The missionaries are having a play," she said. "The story of Noah's Ark, it seems."

I echoed her sigh. "Oh, goody."

We stood uncomfortably for a moment, then I shrugged. "Is there much else to do?" When she shook her head, I nodded. "Might as well join in. Maybe there will be snacks."

I found an empty row of seats and Cora nodded when I gestured to them. After a few more minutes, Ella and Maria ran up yelling "Mama!"

I grinned and pulled them into a hug. "Hey! You ladies here for the thee-eh-tah," I said, purposely over-pronouncing "theater."

My mother came up behind them and eyed me cautiously. I just nodded to the other chairs in the row and she relaxed as she found a seat. The girls jostled around until Cora moved down to allow them to sit on either side of me. They hung on my arms, but I didn't mind.

"I didn't think you would be here," Mom said.

Cora caught my look and came to my rescue. "She needs to get out and about at this stage, and there isn't exactly a lot of low-impact options here." She gave me a playful glare. "But soon, it's hiking hills on the beach for you."

"You mean sand dunes?" Ella piped up.

Cora snorted, giving her words an overdramatic flare. "Did you see any sand on our beaches? We don't have sand dunes. We have gravelly hills with scrub grass. Much more challenging exercise."

I tried to suppress my smile as the girls' eyes and mouths got wider with every word she said. They were eating it up and she was playing them, big time.

"Is Nicola strong enough for that kind of exertion?" Mom asked.

"Not yet," Cora said. "But she was in good health and she doesn't seem to be suffering too much from the exposure to the cold and wet. We are taking it easy, to be sure, but she'll be fine."

Mom nodded, and I shot Cora a look. "Are you holding me back?" I asked bluntly.

"A bit, but we want to be sure there is no chance of secondary drowning."

Maria frowned. "You mean Mama could still drown? But she's not in the water."

"Secondary drowning is when you get water in your lungs and don't realize it. Then, if you overexert yourself, you can drown from that little bit of water moving around inside."

I hugged the girls. "Don't worry," I said. "I would be able to feel it before it could hurt me, as long as we take it easy."

Cora frowned at me but glanced at the two kids in my arms and nodded.

"Attention! Attention please!"

One of the older women from the mission group held up her hands to get everyone's attention. "We are about to begin, but, first, let us pray."

I sighed and sat with as much respect as I could while people around me dropped their heads and clasped their hands. I caught a glare from my mother when she heard my sigh.

I bit my tongue through the whole play, smothering my reactions to the watered-down story, the horrid acting, the preachy epilogue. It felt like I was drowning in the criticisms I swallowed. A short, high-pitched giggle escaped when I wondered if my attempted diplomacy would mask any secondary drowning symptoms. It would be just perfect if I died trying not to insult people who would shove their beliefs in my face at every opportunity, telling me how wrong and evil I was.

"God sent the rains to punish man for their sins!" cried the man playing Noah. "Only the righteous are saved!"

My vision washed yellow before I even realized I was angry. I flashed to my interaction with Rán, recalling her words about keeping mankind in line. The heat boiled up in my blood, crawling up my neck and over my ears.

My breath caught in my throat and I struggled to focus on calming down. I counted - chanted, really - from one to six, over and over, as I wrestled my breaths into a steady, slow rhythm.

My mother glared at me again, but I ignored her, staring at a spot of chipped paint on the wall above the make-shift stage. Suddenly, the yellow in my vision cleared and the anger drained out of my head. I gasped, feeling weak and wobbly in the aftermath.

The audience applauded politely when the play finally ended, and I blinked as people around me began to stand and move away. I looked down at the girls and forced a smile.

"Now what should we do?"

Ella cocked an eyebrow at me, obviously disappointed in my lack of observation. "They are having brownies and stuff. Can't we stay for that?"

I grinned. "Of course. I was just checking."

The girls scurried off with my mom right behind them. I took a few extra seconds to get myself together before standing. Cora watched me carefully.

"Are you feeling alright?"

I nodded. "Yeah. Just, this isn't exactly my kind of happy fun time."

Cora frowned but nodded. "We'd better hurry or the snickerdoodles will be gone." She hesitated once more. "Are you sure you're okay? You seemed kind of... off for a minute."

I smiled weakly. "That? That's an old issue, not a new one," I assured her. "Don't suppose you guys have a shrink on the island?"

Cora shook her head. "Nope. Just the elders. They're better, if you ask me."

I nodded absently, making a beeline for the cookies. "Maybe I'll try that."

CHAPTER 11

I walked slowly along the trail near the beach. I could feel the weakness in my legs and chest, and I hated it. I hated myself and my body for it. I needed strength, not this half-sick lethargy in my muscles.

I was trying to sort through all the information I'd gathered from my brief forays among the rest of the villagers. I examined the behaviors that had stuck out at me, looking for candidates who might have used the Ninth Runespell.

None of the missionaries stood out, but I wasn't going to exclude any of them yet. I knew part of that was sheer stubbornness, since most of their storm-based preaching was about how the weather was some kind of punishment from God and you had to be a good little Christian to make the big bad rains go away. I just couldn't let go of the idea that one of them might calm storms to reinforce obedience to their god.

Then there were the villagers. Elizabeth, the girl who ran the library, seemed likely. Her savvy on political and social issues seemed in line with making such a statement. But then, many of the Yup'ik seemed to have that kind of socio-political understanding.

Also, there were a lot of people who didn't want to have to leave their island. Stopping the storms and the erosion they caused would give the people of Storm Bay that much more time before the ocean levels rose enough to force their emigration.

I sighed. There just wasn't any firm evidence to lock in on any one person. Too many had too much at stake for any one to be the obvious choice.

"Are you alright? You're breathing kind of hard."

I glanced over at my mother walking beside me. What was exercise for me had been nothing more than a leisurely stroll for the older woman. I swallowed the bitterness of that thought.

"No, I'm fine," I assured her. "Just too many heavy thoughts in my head."

"Hmm."

Her reply rubbed me the wrong way – it felt patronizing and dismissive. I tried to convince myself that I was reading too much into what amounted to a neutral sound.

We continued walking for a few minutes. I distracted myself by watching the girls run along the water's edge, picking up things that caught their eye.

"You need to stop it, Nicola," my mother said, finally.

"Stop what?"

"You are always antagonizing people."

I shot her a questioning look.

She sighed and pressed her lips together before elaborating. "The missionaries. You intentionally start fights. You aren't respecting our beliefs."

I snorted. "That's hypocritical."

"How?"

"The fact that I exist is against their beliefs. The fact that I have read the Bible and just don't agree with it confuses them. They think anyone who knows the 'word of God' will fall in line with their own brand of Christianity. They approach people as either evil or ignorant, and that disrespects everyone else's beliefs." I shrugged. "It may not be 'nice' or 'polite,' but I'm just calling them on it."

"Just calling them on it?" My mom frowned, raising an eyebrow in a way I knew I'd done a million times. "Do you really think that's all it is?"

I stared into space, trying not to let the anger boil up. "People who don't follow Christianity, in particular, get the death of a thousand patronizing, hateful, snotty comments. Actions, too." I rubbed the small of my back, wishing away the slight ache that was growing there. "People find out you aren't Christian, and they start quizzing you about what you do and do not know. They say they'll pray for you, like believing something else is the same as getting cancer or losing a loved one."

I looked over at her. "So I'm hitting back. So what? If Christians can't take it, they shouldn't dish it out."

My mother scowled. "Christians aren't being rude about it."

I rounded on her. "Bullshit! Christians are just being the type of rude that Christians have made acceptable in our society. They made the rules and everyone else has to live by them, even though it isn't fair, or even-steven, or just. And those rules just so happen to be that it's not rude to preach Christianity, but it is rude to tell them to keep their opinions to themselves."

My mother stepped back, flinching from my anger. For some reason, that pissed me off even more. She pushed and pushed, then couldn't handle the reaction she got just because I didn't give in to her point of view.

Before I could even focus on getting my anger under control, it drained away. I swayed on my feet for a moment, ignoring my mother's accusing gaze. I focused instead on my own breathing.

"Girls!" Mom called out abruptly, her voice trembling. "We should get back."

The girls ran up. "Mama! Aren't you coming, too?"

I looked at my mom who glared back at me. I wanted to push it. I wanted to spend time with my family. But I knew she would just make it a miserable experience, and I wasn't going to turn the girls against her by insisting they stay with me. I just didn't have the strength for that fight right now.

Instead, I smiled at them. "I'm going to get some more air, okay?"

Maria's face fell. Ella pouted.

"You never do anything with us anymore," Ella complained.

Maria took her hand. "It's okay. This happened to my other mama, too. But grandma is much better than the man who took care of me."

They ran off ahead while I fought the sudden tears that filled my eyes. I gasped for breath, trying not to choke on the disappointment and pain.

My mother shot me a dirty look. "You just have to ruin it, every time we spend time together."

The rage flared up again, pushing pain aside. "I suppose you would be perfectly fine if I was just the only one suffering and did so in silence so you could enjoy putting me down?"

She shook her head. "I'm not trying to put you down. Why isn't that good enough?"

I sighed and closed my eyes, biting down on the words. If "putting down" was replaced with "hitting"... No, she'd probably just accuse me of blowing things out of proportion.

Unwilling to keep verbally sparring with my own kin, and unsure of what else to do, I simply stood and watched them walk away, ignoring the tears on my cheeks and the shaking in my limbs.

"Gods, Nicola," I muttered into the brisk wind. "Can you feel any more sorry for yourself?"

I straightened my shoulders and headed back to the tiny house where Cora was waiting with hot tea.

•   •   •

"Nicola. You look well."

I looked up from the book I was reading - a non-fiction about introverts. Catherine stood inside the doorway, shedding her sweater and smiling.

"Hi," I said. "Um, Cora and Mary are out right now..." I wasn't sure how to handle a guest dropping by when the hosts were out. Should I tell her to come back, or was this acceptable to the locals?

"I know," Catherine said, pulling a chair close to the guest bed/couch where I was reclining. "Cora asked me to stop by to see you. Something about shrinking heads?" The older woman leaned forward as she sat down. Her voice got softer, as if she were sharing a secret. "You know that's African lore, right? You are thinking of the wrong continent."

I smiled at the joke. "Um, yeah. I guess." I took a deep breath, putting the book down on my lap. "Well, um."

Catherine sat back and pulled out a crochet hook and a string of yarn. "Take your time, honey." She began adding stitches to what looked like a scarf. "Just start with whatever comes to mind."

I stared at the needle flashing for a moment, then heaved a breath. "I watched Ella's father die from gunshot wounds. He'd gotten in over his head and I was trying to stop him. Instead, I was dragged into his drama. I'm still caught up in it, in a lot of ways."

Catherine's hands froze, and she stared for a moment before the needle began flashing again. "That must have been hard on you. Most people don't have to go through something that serious, so it's hard for them to understand."

I shrugged. "Several months later, I was looking into a situation for a friend and got caught up in a cult. Some heavy shit went down. It messed me up."

The woman paused in her work. "What kind of heavy?"

I ducked my head. "The guy that ran the cult brainwashed and... abused some of the women." I took a shaky breath. "Including me."

Catherine couldn't hide the gasp, though she tried. "That's... pretty serious stuff," she acknowledged. "I take it you've got some baggage from that?"

I nodded. "The guy... the leader, he found out where I lived and took my mom and Ella hostage. He actually slit Ella's throat before I could stop him."

Catherine put her hands and the crocheting down. "Wow, honey. You must have been beside yourself. Did they catch him?"

I shook my head, my eyes still on the string of crochet stitches. "I took him down before the knife finished slicing and beat him so hard he fell into a coma," I muttered. "Last I heard, he's still comatose."

The woman gasped, raising her hand to her chest. "My god!" She shook off her shock quickly. "Not that I think you did the wrong thing, Nicola. He was obviously a bad man."

I raised my eyes to hers. "I let him get to me," I choked out. "And now I have so much anger."

Catherine reached out and grasped my hand. "Oh, honey. Anyone would be angry about that. It's what you do with your anger—"

"Then, a little over a year ago, I killed the man who had told him where to find my family. I beat him, took his gun, and shot him while he lay helpless."

Catherine pulled her hand back. "W-what? Why—"

"It was the third time he'd tried to kill me. I didn't trust the cops to get anything to stick." I took a shuddering breath. "I still have nightmares about it. But the anger is always there."

I opened my eyes, expecting judgment, shock... so many things. What I didn't expect was the tears in the older woman's eyes.

She wrapped up her crochet and set it back in her purse. Then she took both of my hands in hers. "Some people like to say that god or whatever only sends us what we can handle," she said. "That's bullshit."

My eyes widened, surprised at her language as well as her words.

"There's nobody looking out to make sure we can take it before it's dumped on us," she continued. "It's a nice enough way to look at things, so long as you can keep up with the burdens life throws at you." She sighed. "But some people get hit with way too much. Sometimes they suicide because of it. Sometimes they turn to drink or something harder. Then they often get blamed for not being able to handle it. That's a vicious cycle that only tells us we need to shut up and take whatever comes at us."

I was overcome by the degree to which this woman understood. My eyes filled and overflowed before I could even blink.

Catherine continued. "It's always interesting to see what status quo is kept by that cycle, who gets to keep power and control. And those of us that get angry, those of us that fight back – we are criticized the most for not taking some high road."

She clucked and dropped my hands. "As if the situation hadn't already dropped us into the drainage ditch in the first place. Don't let anyone tell you that you don't deserve your anger. The animals get angry when you violate them. We get angry when we are violated, too. And too much violation makes us perhaps too quick to anger, but you've earned the right to it."

I swallowed around my tears. "Fat lot of good having the 'right' does when people think you're just too sensitive."

Catherine nodded. "True. And sometimes, we get angry at the wrong people. Just try to get back to the balance, eventually. Love is supposed to overcome anger, not suppress it. But that goes both ways. People who love you will forgive you. If they don't, they don't."

I flashed a rueful smile. "Well, tell that to my mom. She doesn't get any of that."

The other woman shook her head. "That's likely because she's bought into suppressing her own violations, whether that choice was right or wrong. You protect the system you've thrown your lot in with." She glanced down at the book on my lap. "Now, I think that's enough raw emotion for one day, hm? We can't dig up all the skeletons in just one conversation or we'd have nothing left to talk about. Tell me about that book. I've been meaning to pick it up."

Catherine sat with me, listening to me read aloud and talking about the points the author was bringing up. We argued politely about what introverts needed from life until Cora and Mary returned. My two hosts tried to convince the elder to stay for supper, but Catherine begged off, claiming she had more business to attend to.

I caught her gaze as she left, and she stopped for a moment, then nodded and smiled at me.

"Maybe next time, we can talk about that penis envy stuff that Freud was so convinced women have." With that, she bustled out the door.

Cora and Mary looked as shocked as I felt for a moment, then we all burst out laughing.

CHAPTER 12

I huffed my way to the community center, not bothering to wait for Cora. There was another production from the missionaries going on. The promise of entertainment in any form, and the store-bought cookies and cakes, guaranteed high attendance.

I frowned at the way the missionaries used the Yup'ik, and how the native people used the missionaries right back. The whole thing left a bad taste in my mouth. I mentioned as much to Catherine when I ran into her in the back of the crowd.

"We have to put up with them no matter what," she pointed out. "At least we get something we want out of it."

I bit back a reply, then I was hit with a realization. "It almost sounds like dealing with family," I ventured.

Catherine gave me an unreadable look. "Yeah," she said. "Depends on the family, though."

I nodded, suddenly uncomfortable. I avoided meeting her eyes by scanning the crowd of people in the community center. It never ceased to amaze me how the entire village managed to fit into a single building – and not a terribly huge building, at that.

I noticed that several of the missionaries seemed agitated, but I couldn't see any reason why. I finally turned to Catherine.

"Is there something wrong?" I gestured to a pair of women who were whispering with sharp, frustrated gestures.

Catherine's gaze moved to the women and she gave me a wry smile. "Oh, everyone is in a state today," she said with a conspiratorial tone. "Some are excited, but some are upset." She looked at me smugly. "It's the second coming of Jeremiah. Well, more like the tenth coming."

I frowned, not recognizing the name or its significance. "Who's—"

"He's another missionary," Cora interrupted, coming up alongside of us. "He first showed up around a decade ago, fell in love with us for some reason, and comes back about once a year." She scowled. "We are his pet project, I think."

Catherine snorted in agreement. "And I wouldn't call it love. More like obsession."

"Or a fetish," Cora agreed. "He tends to be exceptionally pushy and annoying. But he travels a lot for his missionary work, and he always starts out a mission talking about his travels. That is, at least, interesting."

I cocked an eyebrow at her. "You like hearing about other places?"

Cora nodded. "Of course. We live here. It isn't a prison. Many of us leave to go to college, or for work. Just, this is home, so many of us come back at some point."

I nodded, acknowledging my own unconscious bias in the question. "I guess I never thought about it like that, but I did pretty much the same thing."

"We'd better grab some seats before it starts," Catherine said. "Jeremiah's first speech usually ends up with standing room only."

I scanned the chairs set up in the open space and spotted Ella and Maria talking with typical kid animation to one of the local teens. We moved that way and grabbed some chairs next to them and my mother. She shot me an unreadable look and I knew she hadn't forgotten our last conversation. I sighed as I sat down, choosing to focus on the girls rather than her.

They both promptly began speaking over each other, telling me about the cool rocks they'd collected along the shore, and a really twisty tree they'd found while exploring the island. They had even peeked at the marine biologists' base camp and research station through the trees when they'd gone to the far end of the island.

I smiled at their exaggerations and laughed at all the right places, still feeling my mother's judgment at my side like an uncomfortably close fire. After a few moments, the girls ran off to grab cookies that were being placed out by one of the missionary wives, her two teen daughters carrying trays beside her.

"It's nice to see you being so open and friendly to them," my mom muttered. "I wasn't sure you'd remembered how to be nice to your own family."

I rolled my eyes. "Really? Maybe it's the way certain family members treat me, Mom." I heaved a breath and closed my eyes for a second. "I'm sorry. That was petty, and I didn't come here to fight with you."

"Well, I know you didn't come to get right with God. So why are you here?" She glared at me with that look that told me she wouldn't let it go.

I shrugged and gave up trying. When my mother got in this mood, she wouldn't be happy until she got blood, and I was too tired to fake humility for her. "Netflix is buffering, so I thought I'd find something else to do until my movie downloads."

Cora snorted at my other side and I shot her a grin. It had been a common complaint with the survivors who had stayed that there wasn't any real internet, only the satellite connection used sparingly in the storage room library.

Our conversation was cut short as a middle-aged man, tall and lean with dark brown hair and an angular but friendly face, stepped to the front of the crowd. He spoke with a booming bass voice that carried through the low hum of conversation.

"We are going to start in a moment," he said. "Please help yourself to some cookies, and coffee and tea. And please, give seating preference to those who have been around for a while or those with illnesses or disabilities. Thank you."

I quirked a brow, surprised by his thoughtfulness. Before I could put my foot in my mouth with a comment, Ella and Maria ran up with cookies – "gifts" – for me, my mother, Cora, and Catherine.

I accepted my sugar cookie with gusto. "Oh, thank you! Did you make this?" I asked Maria.

"No!" she giggled.

I looked over at Ella. "You, then?"

She shook her head, laughing too much to answer.

I flung up my hands. "Where could you have gotten such wonderful treats?"

The girls pointed over at the table and answered over each other. "Over there." "At that table."

I pulled them in close for a hug as they giggled over my silly behavior. "No way. These taste like my girls. You must have made them."

"No!" "We didn't!"

"Did you touch them, then?"

"Yes..." They paused, wondering where I was going with my question.

"So that's why they are so good! 'Cause you are so good!"

They laughed falling against my embrace as the crowd settled into chairs and leaned against the walls along the side of the seating.

I shushed the girls as the man – no doubt this was Jeremiah – moved back to the front of the crowd. There were no more chairs nearby, so I pulled them on to my knees, one on each leg. I was somewhat surprised by how heavy they'd gotten over the last few years. I didn't remember them being so big the last time I'd held them like this.

I frowned, realizing I hadn't held them much since the incident in the wolf's cave. My thoughts skittered away from that memory and I turned to focus on the man before us.

"Late last year," he began with a voice and cadence made for storytelling, "just after I left you wonderful people, I received a Call to travel to Indonesia, where storms ravaged the land..."

• • •

"And, as we prayed for God to deliver us from the terrible winds and rain, the sky suddenly cleared, as if a giant hand had wiped the clouds from the heavens. And the rains stopped, and we were saved!"

The crowd gasped and clapped as Jeremiah dramatically finished his story. The man smiled softly and gestured for them to calm.

"It was not I who calmed the storm," he said.

I sat up as his words sunk in, my jaw clenching.

"Praise God that we were saved, for it was His hand that swept away the hurricane that surely would have killed us all. Our faith was merely a beacon to Him, calling out for His intervention."

I thought back over the stories the missionary had just told, searching for words and phrases that might hint at his holding a Runespell. There was nothing firm, though he was now a very likely suspect in my search.

I began working it over in my head whether I could give this man up to Rán and her sea monsters. He travelled the world bringing aide to people in need, but he also brought religion. The carrot and stick way he proselytized reminded me of Zaro, though Jeremiah seemed to be less of an abuser and more of a zealot. Either way, I couldn't bring myself to be heartbroken over the idea that he might have to be the one to endure Rán's wrath.

I caught myself daydreaming about how that situation might play out when the crowd around me shifted and the low hum of conversation started up again. I wondered if I'd have a chance to speak with Jeremiah alone, but a quick glance showed that there was already a line to talk to the man.

Instead, I decided to put off that conversation until another day. With it being just after the dark of the moon, what were the chances that the blooded moon would occur tonight or the next? If worst came to worst, I'd just try to negotiate more time from Rán and hope she didn't have Cranky eat me.

I caught my mom watching me with a frown. I rolled my eyes when I realized she'd seen me looking for Jeremiah, and she disapproved of my show of interest.

"You look exhausted," Cora murmured beside me. "Are you ready to get back?"

I tightened my grip on the girls and shook my head. "I'm fine for a bit longer," I lied, feeling suddenly dizzy and weak. I forced a smile to my face and turned back to the girls, asking them about the group of young children they'd joined for short homeschool style classes for several days over the last week.

Ella told me about her adventures with mathematics while Maria answered questions about her reading. I calculated how much school the girls had missed over the last year but was instead hit with the realization that my mom had taken over most of the school stuff for us.

I frowned trying to remember how that had happened. Then it hit me. Part of it was the therapy schedule that I had for myself and Maria. The rest had been due to a particularly bad bout of depression that had kept me in the house for days at a time.

I'd almost forgotten about that, but I figured it had been the better part of a month that I'd barely left the house as the memories and guilt from the situation with Bob had swept over me. The feeling of drowning in those memories had only made it worse, and I had quickly spiraled into a barely functioning state.

I glanced over at my mother, a woman who whole-heartedly rejected therapy and considered mental health issues to be something that indicated a core weakness. I wondered if she had resented my breakdown more than I had realized at the time. It would certainly explain part of her hostility and lack of compassion on that front.

I swallowed down the wash of anger that the thought raised. I'd risked my life for the sake of the world on more than one occasion, not that she knew about it. She only saw the effects, and humanity not dying out wasn't exactly evidence.

Not for the first time, I wondered if I should tell her about the gods and the Runespells. If I did that, I'd have to tell her about Jehovah, too, and I didn't see that going over well with her. She clung to her faith; she needed her faith. And I couldn't blame her for that – we all needed something to believe in – or shatter her beliefs, if I could even convince her I was telling the truth.

I sighed as we finally said our goodbyes and I stood to make my way back to Cora and Mary's tiny home. Someday, maybe, people would really understand why I'd done all that I'd done. But that day wasn't going to be today or tomorrow, so I'd have to just endure the situation as it was.

I heaved a sigh as I climbed the steps to the small home and collapsed on the guest bed. "Suck it up, buttercup," I muttered to myself. "It is what it is."

CHAPTER 13

"You want to meet with Jeremiah?" Cora asked, disbelief coloring her voice. "I thought you were pretty well set against the whole conversion thing."

I shrugged. "Yeah."

Her gaze turned sharp. "You aren't going to start a fight with him, are you? Most of us like Jeremiah. He's persistent but much more entertaining than the others. It wouldn't be good for us if you to scare him off or make him mad. Then we'd just have the regular old boring preaching missionaries and their bad plays."

I held up my hands defensively, then bit back the sniping comment that was on the tip of my tongue. Instead, I simply gave my best look of reassurance and held up my right hand with the first two fingers raised. "Scout's pinky promise, I'll be on good behavior," I said.

"Fine. I'll see what I can do."

The next afternoon, I sat down at the old desk and quirked an eyebrow at the man behind it. Jeremiah smiled smoothly and spread his hands in a what-can-you-do gesture.

"The mayor was kind enough to allow me the use of her office," he said. "I was surprised by the formality of your request, Ms. Crandall. Usually, people who want a moment of my time simply show up."

I nodded, trying not to show annoyance at the car-salesman sheen he held up like a mask. Even his aura and energy sparkled a bit too much. The overall effect was that of a freshly minted penny - virtually untouched by the world.

"I just wanted some time to hear about your travels... and your, um, relationship with..." I pointed skyward, suddenly uncomfortable with the words. Calling the deity Jehovah was too unusual and would draw attention. Calling him "a" god would also draw notice but naming him "God" felt too disingenuous.

Jeremiah smiled and nodded. "I understand, my child."

I cringed. Getting named in such a way by someone only a few years older was... weird.

"I was born and raised in Utah. We were one of the few non-Mormon families in Provo..."

I tried not to let my eyes glaze over as the man went on and on over his completely boring, wonder-bread childhood, despite the enthusiasm he had for relating how he'd had a crisis of faith at 16 years old after losing a beloved aunt to multiple sclerosis 20 years after her initial diagnosis.

Jeremiah described in his satiny voice how he had rediscovered his god and decided to spend his life sharing with those so unfortunate as to not have the correct belief in that same god. After nearly an hour of beige anecdotes meant to excite the listener into becoming one of the faithful, he wound down and gazed at me expectantly.

I covered a half-yawn as best as I could, but his expression fell. I rushed to get the conversation back on track. "I'm more interested in how you know what... God wants you to do. How do you know it's him and not just your own thoughts?"

Jeremiah visibly recovered and smiled tightly. "There is a quality to it when God speaks to you. There is no denying that it is Him." He hesitated as if gathering his thoughts. "I won't lie to you; there are often doubts when God speaks to you. It is part of the test of your faith. You not only must follow His words, you must also recognize them as His words."

I frowned. "So we aren't talking about pillar of fire, booming voice stuff, or angels manifesting in the middle of the road?"

The preacher shook his head and smiled patronizingly. "No, God doesn't do that anymore. He counts on His word being well-known enough that He doesn't have to resort to parlor tricks."

I thought about Jehovah growing huge in anger over what had been a mere guess on my part. I nodded. "No parlor tricks. Got it."

The words must have come out a bit on the dry side because Jeremiah shot me a suspicious look. I offered him an apologetic smile.

"What kinds of things does God tell people?" I laughed. "Like, I get that it wouldn't be about breaking one of the commandments. But what are some things that he's told you, for example?"

Jeremiah nodded. "Well, what God tells each person can be quite personal, or at least specific to them." He smiled. "But I get it. It can be intimidating trying to figure all this out. I mean, it's God, right? What does He want with schmucks like me and you, huh? But no one is too small, too minor for Him. No one is insignificant."

"Yes, but does he ever make... odd requests?"

The man frowned. "Like what?"

I blew out my cheeks. "Like doing specific tasks. Like helping or stopping specific people—"

I cut myself off, shaking my head to clear the numbing fog rolling through my mind. I could see the dirty coveralls and missing-toothed grins of the father and son who had kidnapped me just off the Appalachian Trail at Jehovah's order. I nearly missed Jeremiah's response as I struggled with the smothering, drowning sense of helplessness that surged through me.

"—not common, but it has happened. I can't imagine telling someone that it isn't God unless it is very obviously an evil act."

I pulled in a deep breath and held it for several seconds, catching up with what he was saying. "Right. So gray is probably okay."

"Excuse me?" the preacher asked.

"Never mind," I muttered. "I don't know. I need to think about stuff some more."

Jeremiah's expression softened. "It's okay, my child. Encounters with the Almighty can be confusing if you aren't used to it."

"Can we continue this another time?" I asked, standing. "I feel a little under the weather all of a sudden."

The man stood as well, nodding. "Of course. I heard about your terrible experience during the sinking of the cruise ship. Go rest, and come back when you are up to it."

I nodded, but I was already halfway out the door. I needed a calm, dim space to process what had just happened. The faces of the people filling the community center were nothing more than a blur, until my mother's face crystalized from across the room. The ferocity of her scowl hit me in the gut. I barely glanced at the girls working with pencils and sheets of paper at a table filled with children. Instead, I turned and staggered for the door.

I walked the now-familiar path to Cora and Mary's house, feeling dazed and untethered. Catherine passed in front of me and turned to call out a greeting. She took one look at my face and nodded, falling into step beside me.

She accompanied me without a word until I slumped onto the guest bed. Mary and Cora were out, and I was grateful for the unexpected privacy.

Catherine made some tea, moving around the small kitchen space with familiarity. Then she sat next to the bed, pulling out her crochet. The scarf was longer this time, and I stared at the flashing needle for a long moment.

"There's a storm coming," Catherine murmured.

I jerked my eyes up to her face, certain she was pulling one over on me. Instead of humor, I found a sad resignation in her expression.

"W-what do we do?" I asked.

Catherine shrugged. "I recommend staying indoors, but it's up to you."

I rolled my eyes. "Obviously. But—"

The needle froze mid-stitch. "Calm yourself, qat'sqaq. We live in the space between storms here. It is much like the Norsemen lived in the space between winters. Nature rules, and not necessarily on our behalf. We just carve out a bit of what's palatable."

I nodded, sitting back. There was a quiet, enduring wisdom to the words that seeped into my mind.

"So, why do you not spend more time with your family?"

I sighed. This was not the conversation I wanted to have, but something told me I should have it anyways. "My mom and I, we don't really see eye to eye about some things. Mostly religion and therapy."

Catherine cocked an eyebrow. "Therapy?"

I nodded. "My mom thinks you have to be broken to get therapy. I think it's more like a doctor – sometimes you just gotta do the preventative stuff."

"Ah."

"So she gives me a hard time about going to therapy and for putting the girls in therapy after... the thing that happened."

"Hm. And religion?"

I shrugged. "I'm a Norse deistic pagan. She's fundamentalist-leaning Methodist, though I think that's just because there isn't an evangelical church in our hometown."

Catherine nodded. "So you believe in other gods than the Christian one?"

I winced. "I believe in other gods AND the Christian one."

The needle stopped again. "I heard about Christian witches. Is that—?"

I snorted. "Belief doesn't mean 'worship' or even 'like'. Jehovah's been less than godly every time I've spoken to him."

"You speak to God?"

I caught her dubious look and decided to go with the frontal assault. "You speak to salmon spirits?"

The older woman blinked. "Touché." The needle began flashing through the yarn again.

"Of course, I can't just tell my mom that I don't like her god because he's a meanie butt-head when I talk to him. There's nothing in that she would believe. So I have to hedge, and she thinks I don't 'believe' because I just don't 'know' her god like she does." I sighed again. "I hate how people think that, if you know about Christianity, you'll just fall into the faith. Like, they think it's the most logical religion or something. Gods forbid someone just not agree with it."

Catherine nodded, her eyes on the yarn twisted around the needle in a mass that, to my eyes, was indecipherable. But she just stabbed and looped, making more stitches. When she finally spoke, it jerked me out of the mild trance of watching her.

"Or that agreeing with it is less about faith and more about the practical realities of a conquered people."

I jerked my eyes up to her face, but her expression stayed impassive. I frowned. Catherine seemed to walk the edge of supporting the missionaries and the Yup'ik as a Christian people, but with a jaded, almost bitter, undertone that came out at odd moments.

"Yeah, that's a hell of a thing," I murmured after a long moment. "It's odd, though. I never considered that people being able to keep their culture as a new thing until just recently."

Catherine glanced up and grinned. "You've been talking to the younger ones, eh? Elizabeth? She and Cora both have too much understanding of the nuances of the Yup'ik dilemma, but none of the practicality and—" she heaved a sigh— "the exhaustion borne of fighting the hopeless fight for too many years to number."

I nodded. "That is something I understand all too well." I slumped back and sipped at my now-chilled tea.

CHAPTER 14

Ella and Maria ran ahead as I struggled up the steep incline. It really wasn't very steep, but my less active lifestyle of the past week was still preventing me from having my usual energy. The periodic dizzy spells weren't helping either.

I kept one eye on the ground in front of me, mentally counting steps to keep my feet moving. The other eye watched the girls with a wistfulness.

I wanted to run with them. I wanted to play with them. I wanted to pick up a stick and swordfight with them. I wanted to find the optimism that had been slowly seeping away from my soul.

It was all Bob's fault. Bastard had to go and be such a jerk that I'd finally shot him. Sure, he'd tried to end the world and kill me several times. Sure, he'd set a vengeful man on the trail of my mom and Ella. Sure, he'd deserved it. That wasn't the point.

The point was I'd taken that step. I'd made that choice. I'd been the one to soak up the corruption of that act. And I'd known that's what it would be.

But I missed the me that hadn't dealt with years of Bob and the Runespells.

"Mama!"

I pulled my mind from the dark memories and looked at where the girls were staring. A woman was walking towards us. Her gray-streaked brown hair was pulled back into a braid that matched the splotchy slate-and-brown of her bulky suede coat. Her features were far too European to be Yup'ik.

Cora spoke up at my side. "That's Dr. Roane, one of the scientists doing the seal studies."

I nodded as the three of us converged on where the girls stood gently swishing small sticks at the sparse grasses.

"Cora," the woman said, her deep hazel eyes cataloging everything she saw. "What brings you to our facility?"

I frowned at the insinuated accusation. Were the natives of the island not allowed to go near the research facility?

Cora simply smiled. "We have a guest, Dr. Roane. You might remember that your team found her half-drowned after that big storm? She's just getting her energy back and we thought we'd stretch her endurance."

Dr. Roane frowned. "By interfering with our instruments?"

"Oh no," Cora rebutted smoothly. "We just followed her daughters. I guess we went a bit further than I'd realized. I hope we didn't ruin any of your studies."

The woman's shoulders relaxed but her expression stayed neutral. "Not yet." She turned her attention to me. "So you are the drowned rat we found. Nice to see you on your feet. I wasn't sure it was worth the effort to try to save you."

I raised my eyebrows. "Um, thanks."

It struck me as odd that she'd phrased it like that. After all, they'd only let the Yup'ik know about me. Maybe they'd carried me to the village. It was hardly an effort, really. It wasn't like they'd found me in the ocean and helped me to shore.

A furry puppy face flashed in my memory. I wondered if the seal had even been real.

The doctor was asking Cora about the supply ship. The girls were whispering back and forth, eying the woman's coat.

I took a moment to look at it closer. Suede was an odd choice for a seaside life. There didn't seem to be any water or salt damage, though, so I supposed she treated it.

I frowned, realizing that the coat wasn't really suede so much as a very short-haired fur. It looked like the wet fur of an otter, which I was familiar with due to the girls loving videos of baby otters playing.

I couldn't imagine a scientist in Dr. Roane's place having otter skin, though. It seemed contrary to the conservationism that was so much a part of her job.

A rumble from the constant gray clouds above caught our attention. The clouds seemed to be roiling, and I spotted some distinctly darker areas towards the horizon.

"Storm," Dr. Roane said impassively. "We've been tracking it for hours. Better hurry back. It's going to hit hard."

Cora nodded and I herded the girls back the way we'd come. We waved to the doctor as she stood watching us. Then another deep rumble drew her gaze to the clouds.

I turned my attention to the girls, rushing us over the slight hills with patches of evergreens that made up the center and eastern side of the island. The village came back into view a moment before the skies opened up. We hunched our shoulders against the stinging of icy rain blown by strong ocean winds, making our way to Cora and Mary's home near the edge of the village.

I could almost hear the rage of the sea goddess as we struggled to the door of the small home. I thought about the crystal burning cold against my throat. "Not yet, Rán," I murmured. "Give me more time."

• • •

Cora had tea and packets of cocoa with tiny, dehydrated marshmallows prepared within minutes of entering the tiny home. The girls and I had already shed our coats and piled up on the tiny guest bed. The blanket was pulled up to the girls' noses and their body heat stopped my shivering quickly.

I took the tea Cora offered and waited until she'd handed a mug to Mary and settled into her own chair with a hot cup and a wool blanket.

"Is the doctor always like that?" I asked, sipping carefully at the sweet tasting brew.

Cora shrugged. "They are very concerned about their weather tracking equipment. I understand they have pretty delicate calibrations on them. I think they'd rather be on an island with no people, but they also like that they can pop in for supplies without having to call in a supply boat for themselves."

I nodded. "So they like the convenience that comes with having other people around, but not the part about actually having other people around."

"Pretty much."

I hesitated. "She was wearing a very nice coat."

Cora frowned as she nodded. "Yeah, that's the odd thing. Well, one of the odd things. All of the research team has those coats."

My eyebrows raised at that. "Hm. I'd have thought they'd have a problem with animal skins, what with their whole conservation mission." I shrugged. "Maybe they only allow for the killing of cows."

Cora considered that for a long moment. "Yeah, but those coats aren't cow hides."

I stared at her. A feeling came over me, like a pressure that weighed down my spirit. It wasn't like depression or anxiety. I was familiar enough with those.

It was more like the feeling you get at the top of the first hill on a rollercoaster, or during a phone call with the doctor for test results. It was a sense of importance, gravitas. It was as if every one of my senses understood that the next words would be important.

Only Cora never continued her explanation. Instead, Mary asked for more tea, then the girls fell asleep on my lap and I slipped into unconsciousness soon after.

CHAPTER 15

I slouched down in the uncomfortable chair. My mother and the woman who had stepped up as a family councilor watched me. I pretended not to notice.

"This is what I mean," Mom said. "She just slumps down and doesn't talk to us."

The councilor (Julie?) nodded calmly. "I get the feeling that Nicola feels a need to protect herself by closing herself off. She may even feel like she's protecting those around her."

"From what?" Mom flung her hands up, exaggerating the movement. "We are on an isolated island with friendly people all around."

Julie made a calm-down gesture with her hands and pointedly turned to look at me. Mom turned to add her glare to the caring stare.

I snorted as the rhyme cycled through my mind. Care glare stare. Bare stare care glare.

Mom's anger ratcheted up. "Nicola, can't you take this seriously for five minutes?"

I let my head roll back. "I've seen people murdered in front of my face. I've watched monsters come at me. I've been brainwashed in a cult. I've been raped. I've watched my own daughter have her throat sliced open. I've beaten a man into a coma. I've been chased through the woods by a madman. I've confronted and captured an escaped convict. I've watched my best friend shot and nearly die. I've nearly drowned saving a stranger's life." I paused. "And that's just the stuff I've told you about."

I leaned forward, unable to keep the snarl off my face. "Don't tell me when to take shit seriously. I doubt your definition of what is serious and mine are the same."

Julie took a deep breath, the sound cutting off the words bubbling up my throat. "Do you think your mother doesn't understand?"

I sighed. "How could she? What I've been through..."

"You really shouldn't be so hard on your mother," Julie pushed. "Honor thy father and mother."

My eyebrow twitched. "Is that really the best verse for this situation?"

The two other women turned to stare at me.

"What do you mean?" Julie asked.

My mother scoffed at the same time. "What do you know of Bible verses?"

I shrugged. "He who troubles his family inherits nothing in return. Proverbs 11, if I remember correctly."

Mom frowned at me, but Julie pulled out her bible and flipped through it. She stopped on a page and ran her eyes down it. She tapped her finger on a spot and looked up at me.

"Proverbs 11:29." Her gaze slid over to my mother. "I thought you said she wasn't Christian."

I snorted. "Typical."

Mom glared at me. "She's not."

Julie closed the book carefully and took a deep breath. "Then how did you know-"

"The harder you push your religion on me, the more likely it is, in my experience, that I know about your book than you do." I crossed my arms. "You think I have to be some sort of idiot or ignoramus to not be Christian, but the truth is – and there's studies proving this – the more a person studies the bible, the more likely they are to not believe it."

Julie frowned. "I've studied—"

"Let me guess," I interrupted. "You attended a bible study or followed some kind of guide in your studies."

Julie glanced at my mother, as if asking her for help, but I pressed on.

"Those bible studies and guides usually go for the same stuff over and over. You learn about a quarter of the bible really well but ignore the rest." I sat back, slouching down again. "I've read the whole thing, front to back, three times."

The woman cleared her throat. "Well, anyway. Back to the... um, topic."

"Sure." I waved my hand in a half-hearted gesture for her to go on.

Mom hissed, "Nicola!"

"Nicola, you need to show some basic courtesy, at least." Julie looked more comfortable in a position of having the moral upper hand. "You've had a rough few years. Do you think no one else has endured as much? Do you think no one else has suffered?"

My eyes narrowed and my jaw locked in place. "I'm sure they have."

Julie sat back. "You have endured a lot, but it is stuff you can endure. God only gives us as much as we can handle, but He doesn't guarantee it will be comfortable."

I stood up, welcoming the warm rush of anger up my spine. "That's bullshit. I survived. Barely. I technically died twice. I have nightmares and I can barely function some days. If your God gave this to me, I'll gladly shove it up his ass when I return it. And never tell me it's only as much as I can handle, 'cause maybe handling something and surviving something isn't the same damn thing."

I spun on my heel and left the office before the lava could boil over. The sounds of my mother and Julie protesting my words – both in message and word choice – clattered over my ears. I braced myself to control the Berserker-rage.

The heat leached away, dissipating quickly in the chill air. I swayed on my feet, grabbing for a nearby table to steady myself. This sudden draining of the berserker energy was getting really old.

I stood there, trying to breathe steadily as I examined the experience. It was a bit like when Rade had tried training me in the woods along the Trail. Only this was happening faster and left me feeling empty, like something had been stolen from me. Like I was a deflated balloon with my skin left puckered from the absence.

"Nicola?"

I turned in a daze, struggling to focus on the face before me. Catherine watched me with a concerned expression. I shook off my worry and smiled reassuringly at the elder.

"Hi, Catherine. Just trying to figure some stuff out."

The woman nodded slowly. "Why don't you walk me home?"

The request was odd, and I got the feeling it was more an excuse to talk than any need on her part. I nodded and fell into step next to her. She'd been great to talk to so far. Certainly better than Julie.

The elder was surprisingly spry and I could feel the slight strain of keeping up with her. We walked in the opposite direction of Catherine's home, toward the beach. When only a few houses remained between us and the sea, Catherine slowed her pace and began speaking.

"You don't like the missionaries, do you?"

I shook my head, though she didn't seem to need an answer.

"Neither do I, though I doubt it's for the same reason." She glanced over at me. "You don't particularly like Christians in general."

I pressed my lips together. The question in her pause grew with each step.

"I have had some experiences that—" I considered how much to tell the woman. "I don't much care for—"

I bit back the words and shook my head. My feelings about Jehovah were a rabbit hole that I didn't want to start down. The problem was, it was literally unbelievable what I'd been through. Explaining the unbelievable was not as much fun as it sounded.

Catherine turned to look out over the waves. She stood watching the horizon for a long moment. When she spoke again, I had to strain to hear her over the wind.

"We have lived here for hundreds of years. The wind and the waves, the storms and the invasions – none of it has chased us away. Now, we have climate change and the waves move up the shore, closer to our homes."

She turned to face me. "The missionaries don't always say it, but, after so much time, I've learned what they believe, what they are preaching to the people here."

I followed the woman when she began strolling along the shore, both of us kicking at loose pebbles as we went.

"They believe we aren't right with God. They believe that we are cursed for that. They believe our homes are being destroyed for our sins." She met my eyes with an intense look. "They believe we are Sodom and Gomorrah, being destroyed by God as an example to other villages on other islands."

"That's ridiculous," I bit out.

Catherine nodded. "Perhaps. But that is the story they are selling us to get us to buy their new and improved version of Christ." She stopped and turned to face me. Her expression became even more intense. "That's why the storms are so bad. But, if the storms stop, they say it is God's mercy. He sends the storms to punish us, and He stops the storms as a mercy."

I shook my head. "That would be cruel if that's what was happening. Constant threats withdrawn at a whim. That would be abuse from a parent. From a god, though..." I sighed.

Catherine nodded. "And if it isn't God who is stopping the storms? What if it's some...savior who gets no credit?"

I snorted. "In my experience, saviors don't get credit. Ever. Pain, yes. Credit, no."

The elder sighed and continued down the beach. "Either way, stopping the storms only delays what is coming. Either way, our way of life is ending. We are just borrowing time, now. For ourselves and for the island."

"For the island?" I asked.

Catherine nodded. "Storm Bay Island will be swept under the sea within 20 years, or close enough to it. The island, the village, the forest, even the research station." She caught my startled look. "That's why Dr. Roane gets so testy about any delays. They won't have the time to redo their research here."

I stopped, staring into the trees between us and where I thought the research station was. "That must be hard on them. Grants and data – all at risk because of the storms."

Catherine sighed. "Everyone on the island has a reason to celebrate each storm that stops before it does any real damage." She turned back to her walk. "Now, why are you so angry with your mother today?"

CHAPTER 16

I watched Catherine with dread filling my gut. She simply stared down at her crochet, though I noticed how slowly the needle moved compared to earlier.

I still couldn't believe that I'd told her so much. It was the Cliff's Notes version of what had happened with Bob and Keith, and Zaro and Nancy, but it was still a lot. It was a lot of weird crap, but also so much unbelievable crap.

I'd told her about running from demons. I'd told her about becoming addicted to the astral plane. I'd told her about the Berserker lurking within me.

Her needle flashed for another minute of silence before she finally put it down and looked at me.

"Just because I believe in spirits and such doesn't mean I can just completely believe you."

I nodded and reached for a lighter that Cora used to light emergency candles when storms took out the power. I glanced up to make sure Catherine was watching, then clicked on the lighter and used the seventh Runespell to make the flame dance in time to my rough singing of the Macarena.

The older woman covered her mouth with one hand, her eyes getting wider as the flame gyrated.

I let the lighter click off and waited.

"Oh," she whispered, then uttered a string of syllables that I couldn't understand.

I frowned as I tried to pick out something that made sense to me in the sounds, and she cut off suddenly.

"I'm sorry," she said. "I didn't need to overreact like that."

I raised an eyebrow. "That was overreacting? I only wish my friends had done so little. Instead, I got a lot of push back about what I had to do."

Catherine nodded. "I can see why." She raised her hand when I opened my mouth to protest. "I'm not saying I agree with them. Just that I understand why."

I considered that for a brief moment before nodding. I could see why Joseph had gone the route of pushing me to be the Hero(tm), though it still frustrated me.

I realized now that most of that frustration was that I absolutely agreed with him. I wanted to be the Hero(tm), but it simply wasn't that kind of clean-cut situation. I desperately wanted it to be, but there was mushiness and that meant I couldn't just do the "right thing" all the time. I couldn't be the Hero(tm) because heroes were too perfect for real life.

I sighed. "Yeah."

Catherine spoke hesitantly. "I guess what it comes down to is, what do you think of what you've been through?"

I sat back, thinking over the question. "I don't know. I—" I bit my tongue, knowing I was going for the moderation, the acceptable lie. "No, I hate it. I hate what I'm becoming. I hate the anger and the violence. And I hate that I feel so helpless about it. I don't seem to have a choice in any of it. And I hate that the gods I respect are the ones manipulating me in all of this."

The woman nodded, picking up her crochet once again. "That's reasonable." She glanced up at me before continuing. "Have you considered that the whole situation isn't what you think it is?"

I frowned. "What do you mean?"

"Well, you get visits from gods and demons, right? Why are you so sure that they all are who they say they are?"

I swallowed hard. A tiny thread of fear that had been growing over the past few years burst into bud. What if I was wrong? What if all this was some trick? I'd based my faith in what I was doing on two unproven facts – that gods, like fae, couldn't outright lie – and that I could discern their word games if they tried to get around the truth.

But even if the first was true, I'd already been fooled by the Norns. They had implied things about themselves and about Hel that turned out to be completely inaccurate. I'd avoided thinking about it because it wore away at the foundation.

That foundation was what I'd based my actions on. That foundation was why I'd killed Bob.

"Dammit," I muttered.

Catherine nodded. "That's what I thought. We need to check in once in a while to make sure we aren't crazy."

I sighed. "I haven't known many people who have these kinds of experiences who can understand that. I'm usually too busy defending my perceptions to question them."

"That's the dangerous part," Catherine said. "That's when we dig ourselves in to that belief so much, we have to keep defending it, even against ourselves."

"It becomes the hill we die on?"

She nodded and I watched the needle move for a long moment.

"I can prove the Runespells are a thing, that they have power, but everything else..." I shrugged. "I have to believe it, or I have to admit I'm the bad guy."

Catherine peered up at me for a moment. "We can't let that be the reason. We can't keep from being the bad guy if we never call that into check."

I nodded. "You're right. I'm just not sure how to do that. It all comes across as self-accusation and justification."

She nodded. "Indeed it does."

• • •

The land itself reflected the spirit of the island I was on in the physical. The stark rocky ground bordered sharp-branched trees and spiney bushes. All of them were colored a brighter green than they showed in the physical world, reflecting the life they hid from human sight.

The aggressive forest and barren beaches gave way to a maelstrom of blues and greens. The sea was even more active here, with the waves reaching out with hand-like projections that clawed at the shoreline.

Among the swirling colors of the water, even more amazing creatures swam. Fish with huge mouths leapt into the air and stalked other creatures, which in turn stalked their own prey. Tendrils and veil-like fins ringed heads and tails in a way that their physical forms never showed.

Cat-like seals swam with webbed feet instead of the fins they would normally have, and giant whales gnashed teeth and puffed-up pouches to be even more intimidating than the ostensibly gentle giants of the oceans were.

I watched as the life teemed in front of me, clearly visible despite the waves. The reflections here were more akin to the animals' personalities than their physical forms were, and the difference was striking.

It had been months since I'd come into the astral plane. It felt like a former home – familiar yet strange, like everything was in the wrong place.

I closed my eyes and thought of the conversation with Catherine. I needed answers, and I wasn't sure where else to go.

The question bloomed in my mind. *What is the truth?*

I felt the world shift around me, a faint carsickness of motion without my body moving. I opened my eyes and scowled at Jehovah's Garden.

"Why the hell am I here?"

"You tell me." The smooth voice crawled up my neck, the seduction in it making my stomach turn.

I craned my neck around, then turned to face the devil. "Hey, Lucy. I'm home!"

The handsome man quirked his lips in a faint smile. "Nicola, Nicola, you always entertain me."

I folded my arms over my chest. "Well doesn't that just complete me. I'm supposed to be finding the truth. Am I supposed to believe that I can get that out of the Father of Lies?"

Lucifer shrugged. "Perhaps. I don't really lie so much as play with the truth. Like silly putty."

I rolled my eyes. "Where's your so-called better half?"

He scowled. "Don't start that again, Nicola. We were getting along so well."

He took a step forward using his larger body to his advantage. I refused to back up.

"I saw you," I said firmly. "I saw Jehovah turn into you."

Lucifer rolled his eyes. "You think you saw that. I don't know why you would have, but it isn't the case. I am not Jehovah."

I shook my head. "Whatever. What is Jehovah doing on the island?"

He took a step back, giving both of us more space. Those handsome eyebrows rose, creating lines in that perfect forehead. "Island? You mean that little dollop of land in the middle of the sea?"

It was my turn to roll my eyes. "Yeah, that's what an island is. Why does Jehovah have missionaries there? Is one of them working for him? Are all of them working for him?"

Lucifer rubbed his chin. "I don't think so. I haven't heard anything about that. But I'm not exactly in God's inner circle, if you understand my meaning."

I gritted my teeth. "Then I want to talk to him."

Lucifer turned, calling back over his shoulder. "Then I'll leave you to face Him." He faded, going transparent until he disappeared entirely. His voice rang out in the empty space. "Good luck..."

I scowled. "I don't need luck!"

"No, you don't. But manners might help."

I spun around as the calm voice sounded at my side.

CHAPTER 17

Jehovah stood with his hands tucked into his billowy sleeves. His long beard hung down behind the joined sleeves, but his eyebrows were drawn together in an expression of disapproval.

I considered a sarcastic retort. It would certainly be what he expected from me. Instead, I heaved a sigh and simply watched him for a moment.

The turnabout of calm examination seemed to throw him off, and his eyes darted away a few times before he managed to recenter himself. I watched him regain his self-control with as neutral an expression as I could manage. I waited until his mouth twitched before I spoke.

"I don't want any of your stupid games," I said, keeping my voice low and calm, but firm. "I just want to know one— no, two things."

I held up a finger when he opened his mouth to speak. "One: did you arrange for the ninth Runespell to land in the hands of any missionaries on the island where I'm currently staying?"

Jehovah frowned and pressed his lips together before he responded. "Not that it's any of your concern what I do with my flock…" He hesitated a moment before continuing. "But no. I did not."

I sighed. It was the answer I'd expected, but I had hoped he might give another.

He watched me closely for a long moment. "You don't believe me."

I shrugged. "It doesn't matter. I have your response on record. That's all I wanted." I held up a second finger before he could respond. "Second, what was your name before Jehovah?"

The god blinked. His mouth opened before he could stop himself, but he cut off any sound that might have come out. He swallowed and frowned at me as I pulled out the chain filled with Runespell pendants.

"I have learned the fourteenth spell," I intoned. "If I want to, I shall know, by name and function, every god and demigod and creature of the gods; I know all their stories, while others know only a few."

I focused on Jehovah as the Runespell went cold. I saw his eyes widen into an expression of horror. Then the images crashed into me.

It wasn't dissimilar to the way the pearl of implanted knowledge from Huginn and Muninn had come into my mind. The jumble of visual and audio quickly overwhelmed my senses. I flinched back. Never had the knowledge of the fourteenth Runespell been like this.

I struggled to find something in the mass of sensation that I could anchor on to. Instead, my mind swirled until it split into three distinct arms of a spiral galaxy. One of those arms split again, and a second split immediately after. The second split arm split again, and the entire windmill faded from my consciousness.

Part of my mind struggled with what happened for a moment before I felt myself fall back into my physical body. Laying on the bed where I'd been when I went to the astral plane, I opened my eyes for a moment, glad I was at least not incapacitated as I'd been with the raven's pearl of knowledge.

I stared at a spot on the wall, focusing on my breath in an effort to get my thoughts in order. Finally, the racing images slowed, and I let the exhaustion come over me.

• • •

I took a deep breath. "The day after tomorrow? That seems... fast."

Cora nodded. "Yeah, the coast guard tends to take search and rescue pretty seriously. Even if they are late to the party."

I frowned, staring at the door. I'd noticed that the moon was getting bigger and bigger. The crystal burned ice-cold on my chest and I knew Rán wouldn't wait another month. With the full moon in a few days and the coast guard coming to pick up the remaining survivors of the sunken cruise ship, my time had nearly run out.

That didn't change the fact that I was barely able to spend a few minutes in the same room as my mother, or that I still had no idea if the Runespell was even on the island, never mind who might be using it. I could see the waves of consequence rising up to crash over me.

"Nicola?"

Cora's voice broke through my thoughts, but the water still covered me, blurring everything. Then I felt her hand on mine.

"Why are you crying?"

I realized the burning blur over my vision was tears. I blinked and they streamed down my cheeks. I tried to speak, but my throat had closed.

I wanted to ask questions, get to the bottom of things. Instead, I cried. A rough keen tore at my vocal cords, stealing away my words.

Thoughts raced through my head – Keith and Bob, Nancy and Zaro, Ella and Maria, Joseph, Mercy. All the abuses I'd seen and suffered through hit me at once. Mostly, it was the thought that I was tired, that I didn't want to do it anymore, that it was all too much.

Cora pressed a tissue into my hands, and I blew my nose over and over, clearing away my angst with the mucus.

"Thanks," I whispered as the tissue was replaced with ice cold water. I sipped at the cup, blinking eyes swollen with my tears. A moment later, a washcloth landed in my lap.

I glanced up and gave Cora a wobbly smile. I wet the cloth with the cold water and pressed it to my eyelids. The relief was instant. I could feel the pressure leaving my face as I sat there, head tipped back.

A few more sips and two more wettings of the washcloth later, my voice came back. "I need to figure something out. I'm running out of time, and people might die if I can't." I looked up at Cora. "Who would benefit from these storms going away?"

Cora blinked. "Going away? The storms? Wait – who might die?"

I shook my head. "I don't know. Just... who benefits?"

Cora blew out her cheeks. "Well, most everyone might benefit some. It depends on the situation and how they might spin it, I guess. I mean, pretty much everyone would benefit."

I shook my head. "I was afraid you'd say that." I reached for a notebook and pen sitting nearby. "Okay, let's go through this, step by step."

Cora shrugged. "Okay."

I scribbled on the paper. "Missionaries. Any one in particular?"

"I guess Jeremiah. He likes those dramatic miracle stories. But he hasn't been on the island very long. What time period are we talking about?"

I shrugged. "Maybe a week or more before the ship sank. How did Jeremiah get on the island anyways?"

Cora's mouth quirked. "He has his own private boat and a guy who pilots it. His name is Tommy. He likes to think that this is his private retreat just because he was born here."

"Really?"

"Yeah, but his family moved to the mainland when he was still a kid."

I wrote down names and some brief notes. "Any other missionaries?"

"I guess Martin is the pushiest. He's the one who lead the class on the Jonah story." Cora's eyes glittered with her humor. "You know, the one you upset."

"'Kay." I scribbled some more. "Any more stick out?"

"Not really."

"Hm. How about villagers?"

Cora sighed. "Any one of us would benefit."

I nodded. "Okay. Then who might actually pull the trigger on something like that?"

"That's a different issue," Cora admitted. "Traditionalists might say that the spirits want the storms and we shouldn't interfere. Realists might say that we can't fight global warming forever." She shrugged. "But then traditionalists might also decide that if we can stop it, it is the spirits helping us, and the realists would take any mitigation of the erosion as that much more time before we are forced to leave."

"Okay. But who, specifically, would have the personality to pull the trigger?"

She frowned and shook her head. "There are a lot of people with strong opinions and even more with strong character. You don't last long on an island just south of the Arctic Ocean unless you have some deep running inner strength."

"So anyone who steps up with strong opinions or as a leader is a definite yes?"

"I guess."

Cora appeared discomforted by the conversation. I sighed.

"Sorry," I offered. "It's not fair of me to have you judge your own community like that."

She shook her head. "I'm just not used to thinking about my people, my neighbors, in that light." She chewed on her lower lip for a moment. "Elizabeth would be one of the realists. She's probably the most aggressive."

"Thank you." I reached over and awkwardly patted her arm. I tried to hide any disappointment about not having any real new information. "What about the traditionalists?"

"Well, there's Tommy. And Stephen might, too," she said, hesitating before continuing. "He hasn't been around much. He doesn't like the missionaries, so he makes himself pretty scarce when they are here. He's probably been busy trying to get more work from the research station."

"The research station?" I asked. "What kind of work?"

Cora shrugged. "Mostly, he pilots his boat as a small supply ship for whatever we or they need. He can't get everything we need, but he's faster than the regular supply ship. He also does some maintenance work for people around the island. The researchers also sometimes have him pilot them out into the ocean for data collection."

"Hm. Anyone else?"

"Well, there's the elders, of course. Grandmama and Catherine are probably the most outspoken. The rest are pretty fatalistic about natural disasters."

I sighed. "Still so many to pick from. I've definitely got my work cut out for me." I glanced toward the door once again. "I think I'll go for a bit of a walk and see what comes to mind."

Cora's eyes narrowed slightly, and I knew she didn't quite believe my outing would be just an innocent walk. But I didn't offer anything more and she didn't ask.

CHAPTER 18

It took me only a few minutes to make my way to the community center. It was as bustling as it had been all week, with missionaries in black slacks or dark skirts mingling with the more casual jeans-wearing villagers.

I slipped in without anyone appearing to notice me and looked around. It had been so long since I'd relied on my own power to do anything, really, but the years of practice made it easy to get back into the mindset.

A few deep breaths and I let my eyes relax, willing my mind to perceive the energies that filled the world around me. At first, there was little more than a few spots of color overlaying "reality." Then I began to see images, like the afterimage from staring at a shape then looking at a blank wall. The difference was that the images I saw moved as I watched them, slipping in and out of view.

I didn't focus on the images, though. Instead, I pulled up the feeling of need and no small amount of desperation that I felt about finding the Runespell and whoever held it. I let the feeling roll around in my head, emotions and thoughts mingling into a ball of energy that represented the need itself.

I closed my eyes and felt the pressure in my gut as I propelled the energy into the world. I breathed through several seconds of waiting, giving the energy a chance to do its work. Then I opened my eyes.

The problem with spells like this one was that it often showed strong possibilities, not just the right answer. That was one of the things that made real spell work less effective for practical investigation. I couldn't ignore the possible advantage it might give me though, even if it was more of a shortcut than an answer.

I opened my eyes and let my gaze wander over the crowd. A slight glow caught my eye and I spotted Jeremiah talking animatedly with a young man in a flannel shirt and a ponytail.

I moved closer, hoping I wouldn't be rudely interrupting a private conversation. The young man glanced at me, which drew Jeremiah's attention. The preacher turned toward me.

"Nicola, right?"

I nodded.

"I was just telling Samuel here about that storm in Indonesia." Jeremiah smiled at the youth. "He missed the first telling, but we won't hold that against him." The preacher reached out and gently nudged Samuel's arm to show he was joking.

I nodded politely. "Yeah, I was hoping I could hear some more details about that." At Jeremiah's look, I continued. "You probably tell it so much, you focus on the exciting parts. I wanted to know more about your prayers. Do you use a rosary or something when you pray?"

Samuel seemed a bit tongue-tied but looked at Jeremiah with interest. I knew the preacher wouldn't be able to resist the possible conversion of both of us.

"I don't," he said. "I know many who do, and Catholics, of course, but I do not let anything represent God the Father, lest it become my idol."

I nodded. "So no special necklace or anything that you can touch to help bring that connection closer?"

Jeremiah smiled and I gritted my teeth against the patronizing look he gave me.

"I need only my bible," he assured me. He turned his head to include Samuel in his look. "You could be naked, stripped of all your worldly belongings, and God would hear you as if you were in your Sunday best and kneeling before an altar in church. The church is His house, but He is not restricted to that."

"'The Kingdom of God is within you and all around you'," I muttered, drawing a sharp look from Jeremiah. I ignored him and finished the quote. "'Split a piece of wood and I am there, lift a stone and you will find me.'"

"I like that," Samuel said, finally breaking his silence.

Jeremiah frowned. "It's pretty and poetic, and it sounds like the words of Jesus, but it isn't." He focused on me. The intensity of his gaze was intimidating. "What is that from?"

I shrugged. "Gospel of Thomas, or the movie 'Stigmata'..." I barely caught the brief sneer that flashed across Jeremiah's face at my words.

"That's heretical," he declared.

"Gnostic, actually," I said. "Though more evangelical types don't distinguish between the two."

"And that's a problem for you?"

I shrugged. "Just wondering why someone who isn't Catholic would be so married to the idea of the bible as the be-all, end-all when all that was decided by the Pope and the very Catholic Councils of Nicaea. I mean, if you aren't going to follow the Pope, why does he get to decide which words of Jesus are canonical and which aren't."

Jeremiah's face flushed red and he pressed his lips together.

I nodded. "You aren't the droid I'm looking for, I'd guess."

Before he could respond to the reference, I turned on my heel and walked away. I made a beeline towards the other missionaries that I'd noticed. Martin was holding court of some kind with a small group of villagers and missionaries. I smiled when I realized that the kids were drawn to the heaping plate of cookies and brownies he held hostage.

I slipped into the back row of people forming loose arcs in front of him. His wife, Julie of the family counseling, frowned at me but said nothing when I simply watched.

"—why the story of Noah is so important. God will never let the world drown again. The rainbow is his promise."

One of the older boys scowled. "We don't usually see rainbows. It's too overcast most of the time."

Another boy, much younger, gaped at that. "Does that mean God doesn't promise US?"

Martin shook his head. "Of course not! God's promise was for everyone. Even if we don't get to understand His will, He loves us all."

"But the storms are going to take the island," the younger boy said. "Doesn't God want us to be safe?"

Martin squatted down and several of the kids took advantage of the easy access to the desserts. "God wants you to be safe. That's why He sent us to help you move to the mainland. It will be different, but it will be safe."

The older boy scowled. "What about the storm that sunk the cruise ship?"

Martin nodded. "God doesn't keep us from experiencing natural disasters and pain. He just promised to never flood the whole Earth again." He calmly met the older boy's gaze and held out the plate for him to take a cookie.

Reluctantly, the boy snatched one of the baked goods and scowled while taking aggressive bites out of it.

"So, you don't think that God sends messages to people through natural disasters?" I asked, drawing the attention of most of the crowd.

Julie's eyes narrowed at me, but she merely pressed her lips together while her husband responded.

"I think God's actions are more subtle than they were in the Old Testament. He prefers us to look with our hearts, with love, not with fear of what He might do to punish us." Martin's expression was too patronizing to not annoy me.

"Based on most Christian groups, the fear of hell and damnation is exactly what is supposed to motivate them," I pointed out. "Some of you even prefer sermons that are referred to as 'Hell & Brimstone' preaching."

Martin nodded. "True, but His followers are not necessarily a reflection on God. Unfortunately."

I snorted. "Too bad all y'all insist that you are the truest reflection. Can't all of you be right."

Martin shrugged. "We all must find our own way—"

I barked a laugh. "As long as it's the one true way. And you can help us find that one, right?"

Julie scowled as she stepped forward. "Nicola, we are all aware of your hatred of Christians-"

"Wrong!" I snapped. "I don't hate Christians. I hate people like you pushing your religion down other people's throats. I hate you bribing kids with cookies to listen to your indoctrination. I hate you using people's situations to strong-arm them into your faith just because somewhere along the line you got it all in your head that belief was a numbers game."

I felt the warmth of anger crawling up my neck, but it didn't take hold the way it had years before. While I was glad to not have to struggle for control of myself, it was more concerning than it was a relief.

"You go ahead and force conversion. Just don't blame me for laughing on the sidelines when your savior doesn't appreciate your less than loving and selfless approach." I spun on my heel again and headed for the door.

I wasn't completely convinced none of the missionaries could be using the Runespell, but I was also becoming anxious. Too many people that I felt I needed to argue with. Too many fronts to fight on. And my one ace in the hole, my berserker, seemed to have been left on the bottom of the ocean with Cranky the Kraken.

CHAPTER 19

I wandered out onto the beach along the edge of the village. Cora had been right. It wasn't really a beach so much as a stretch of rocks worn down to gravel. I kicked at a bit of grass that had poked through the stones and stared out across the water.

On many levels, I knew I was more broken than I should be, but I also was at a complete loss as to what to do about it. All of my experience and knowledge was either useless or took too much energy for me to push through it by myself, or was just not what I needed. Maybe.

I thought about what my therapist had told me, but I kept running into the fact that she didn't know about so much of what I'd been through. Patient-doctor privilege didn't extend to admissions of homicide, even if the guy had deserved it. Spending time on a court case to prove it had been self-defense would not be helpful to me, my kids or the stupid quest for the Runespells.

I also thought about just dumping my issues at the feet of the gods who had created this situation for me. Odin and his little mind-games, the Norns being all creepy to keep me unbalanced so I wouldn't question them too much, and Jehovah and his Satan aspect. Or was it the other way around?

Gods! I wished I could just get a straight answer.

One of the pendants at my neck burned as cold as the gem that Rán had placed there. Information flooded my mind, details of the gods that no mortal had known in centuries. Or maybe ever.

Odin's favorite color? Oh, yeah. That was enlightening. Tyr's words to Fenrir before the chain snapped on? Well, the detail is nice, but it didn't really help now, and wouldn't have when I was face-to-face with the monstrous wolf. It certainly wouldn't have helped in my fight against good ol', nasty ol', dead ol' Bob.

The information on Jehovah and Satan was much more useful, but still not what I needed to get my metaphorical feet under me. I mean, yeah, Jehovah disappeared for centuries, then re-emerged with the Satan nemesis when the Judaic god hadn't had a direct enemy before.

So helpful.

Stupid Runespells were more trouble than they were worth.

I could see why people would use them more to try to end the world than to save it. If the knowledge of how crappy people and gods could be when everything was on the line was the price of such power, I'd be returning that gift still in the box.

I let the knowledge I'd unintentionally summoned wash over me. It seeped into the back of my mind, but I refused to focus on it too much. Too much of my time had already been stolen by this quest.

I promised myself that, if the situation ever arose again, I'd tell any gods that wanted me to be all heroic to shove it up their divine asses.

With that promise to myself firmly in my mind, I turned to stride across the beach to search out the mysterious boat captains that Cora had mentioned. Neither one seemed particularly promising, but neither did any of the others.

I recognized that I was avoiding confronting any of the Yup'ik people about using the Runespell, but I promised myself that I'd get to it sooner rather than later and kept walking.

It didn't take long before I realized that I had no real idea where to find the boats or their captains. I assumed it would be along the coastline, which wasn't insignificant. Sure, you could hike around the whole island in a day if you pushed yourself, but I was still not at peak condition. Truthfully, I'd never really been at peak condition, but I was even less so now.

I decided to just walk until I found something or got tired. I meandered over various types of gravel and rock along the shoreline, moving in toward the trees when the rocks got to be too much like mountain climbing for comfort.

After the first half hour, the residual anger and anxiety I'd been feeling left, and I felt weary and empty. My purposeful stride became more of an amble in the general direction of the next marker I'd picked out on the shore.

There were a few sharp corners in the shoreline, where an inlet or a jut of land created more of an angle then the slow curve of the beach required. It was at one of these that I stumbled through a patch of brush and staggered to a stop in front of a worn pier jutting out into the water.

Two decent sized boats bobbed along the wood planks. Each was painted in a pattern of black and white with accent colors edging the sides. The covered central part of the boats took up most of the deck with only the last third left open.

I stared at the vessels for a long moment, wondering what to do next. The craft that was closer seemed more well-kept with yellow and blue accents, named "Hannah's Promise." The other, with green and red accents, was positioned so that I couldn't see the name painted on the side of the vessel.

As I watched, a middle-aged man walked out of the covered portion of "Hannah's Promise" and stood with his legs spread for balance, staring at me.

"C'n I help you?" he called.

"I hope so," I yelled back. "What's your name?"

"Stephen Imgalrea. Who's asking?"

"My name's Nicola," I said. "I'm from the cruise ship."

The guy frowned and moved to the opening along the side which allowed him to step off the boat onto the dock. "I'm not planning a trip to the mainland until next week, if you're lookin' for a ride."

I shook my head, stepping closer to the boat. "Not today," I assured him. "I was just hoping you could tell me more about the storms."

He scratched at his shaggy hair and scowled. "Storms? What's there to tell? The sea has storms. They been getting worse. Sometimes they break stuff. Sometimes they stop sudden-like. That's it."

I glanced away from his hard stare, unsure how to push further. If I outright asked, he might think I was crazy and not give me any information. But if I was too vague, I wouldn't get what I needed. "You ever notice anything... strange? When the storms stop suddenly, I mean."

He shrugged. "I dunno. Sometimes it seems more... natural, I guess you'd call it. Other times, it's like some kind of force makes it happen." He stopped and cleared his throat. "O' course that's just natural stuff we don't really understand, though, right?"

I nodded, considering his words. He didn't seem to have any information I could use. I was already thinking ahead to my next stop and nearly missed what he said.

"... damn seals."

I blinked. "What about the seals?" I wondered what anyone could have against the adorable but avoidant sea mammals.

"Used to be you couldn't hardly find a one of 'em around here. Now they seem to pop up any time I gotta make a run. The gals at the research station think the seals claimed territory to the northwest, and that's right on my route."

I frowned. "Why is that a problem? Do they get in the way?"

The man shrugged. "Not so's I can't avoid 'em. Just make me go outta my way. Couple of times, goin' around put me into a storm path."

I frowned. "Are you saying the storms avoid the seals?"

He shrugged again. "I ain't sayin' what storms do and do not. I'm saying they got the best spot to be in the last few blows. Probably some weather sense. Or spirits."

I raised my eyebrows at that.

Stephen scowled at my expression and huffed. "Don't you be makin' assumptions. I got a clean head on my shoulders, but sailin' these waters makes you appreciate that there's stuff you just can't see or explain."

I nodded. "I get it. Trust me on that."

Abruptly, the sailor turned and boarded his boat once more. I stood for another moment, not sure how the conversation had ended so suddenly.

"Thanks!" I called, not sure what else to say.

The man lifted a hand without looking up.

After another awkward moment, I turned and continued up the shoreline.

CHAPTER 20

It took me another hour of huffing along the beach before I came to the conclusion that I was not going to reach the research station before nightfall. I stopped and sat on a fallen log for several minutes, in part catching my breath, but mostly feeling sorry for myself.

I realized a part of my problem was that I really just wanted the whole thing to be easy. I'd already done so much for the greater quest, I should be able to handle these little issues better. Instead, it was just wearing on me.

I thought back to how overwhelmed I'd been during that first situation in Indianapolis. Meeting Mercy and the ravens. Facing down monsters and demons. Coming to terms with the complexity of my relationship with Keith.

It had been too much. I'd seen people die in front of me, but I'd always had to keep moving. No time to mourn. No time to process. Even the big breakthrough had been an overwhelming sensory experience that nearly killed me.

That thought brought back memories of my time with the Hands. A healing cult that had literally killed me, and that had nearly killed my family. Yet I couldn't remember most of my time with them. I'd spent so many days out of it, under the influence of their brainwashing and the Runespell's temptation.

I shivered at the vague memories I still had of that. The loss of control. The loss of consciousness on my part. I hadn't just had control taken from me, I'd given it up freely for a few good feels.

The shame washed over me when I remembered those I'd failed to help, the abuses I'd failed to stop. The nightmares still came back occasionally, though they had slowed significantly after Bob...

I stood up suddenly, unwilling to go through the memories of my final encounter with the fanatic Bob and his attempts to stop me. He'd given me the willies when I first saw him, but by the end I'd known him to be the greater monster even compared to the grotesque demons he'd controlled during our first battle.

I strode into the forested center of the island, determined to outrun those horrors. But the thought still wormed into my head. It wasn't horror I'd felt. It was guilt. And power.

By the time I found my way back to the village and stumbled into Cora and Mary's little house, I'd lost myself in fighting back the memories and the feelings, reliving my worst days over and over, barely aware of my surroundings.

I dropped onto the narrow guest bed and accepted the hot tea that was pushed into my hands, but I couldn't concentrate on the questioning voice the penetrated the fog around my head. I simply shook my head, drained the cup and collapsed into a sleep of both physical and mental exhaustion.

• • •

The sunlight pushed against my eyelids, keeping them shut but waking me all the same. I reveled in the calm I was feeling, sure that it was precious but not realizing why.

Then the memories came back. All of the nasty horrors of my previous day's trip into the past came crashing back into my mind. I grasped for the pleasant calm even as it fled, and I was left shaking with the need to cry over my pain.

I shook myself into full consciousness, berating myself for the nostalgic heartache I had indulged in. I was getting really tired of feeling sorry for myself and the anger began to burn at my ears. I let it grow for several minutes but it soon faded away without a real live threat to keep it going.

I sighed. The berserker in me still didn't have any staying power.

I never thought I'd miss the time I couldn't keep the rage from spilling out. But here I was.

I rolled over, staring up at the low ceiling. I knew I needed to get going. My time was running out. But, without optimism or anger to push me, my motivation was seriously hampered. I argued with my arms and legs for several minutes before they obeyed my orders to move, and I sat up.

Mary was eyeing me from her usual seat, her crochet needle flashing once again. "Sleep well?"

I barked out a laugh. "Not really. But I never sleep well." I considered for a moment. "I do occasionally pass out, though. A lot, recently."

Mary hummed in acknowledgement but did not continue the conversation. That left me the space to reflect on my interviews the previous day.

I was pretty well convinced that none of the missionaries had the Runespell. The boat captain, Stephen, didn't seem very likely either. Between those disappointments and the emotional rollercoaster, I was content to simply sit up on the bed and let the thoughts bang around in my head for a while.

When I did get up and clean myself up for the day, I moved slowly, without real purpose or energy. I plopped down on the bed, ready for anything and nothing to happen. The door was open to the rare sunshine, and I watched the few people out walking around.

After a while, a brunette head appeared around the doorway. My mouth formed a smile before I'd even consciously put a name to the face.

"Mama?" Ella called tentatively. "You wanna go for a walk?"

I saw Maria behind her, and Cora even farther back, but no sign of my mother.

"Sure," I said, jumping up and waving to Mary as I trotted down the steps. "Gramma not coming today?"

The girls shook their heads before grabbing my hands and pulling me forward. I met Cora's eyes over their tousled hair and smiled my thanks to her. She had no doubt noticed that I had sacrificed time with my daughters to try to keep the peace between me and my mom. Not that I'd ever been successful at that.

"Where are we headed today?" I asked.

The girls talked over each other in their excitement, but I deciphered something about a tree and a weird branch. Satisfied with the vague destination, I let them set the pace and pushed myself harder than I would have alone.

My muscles protested a bit after my long walk the day before, but I was surprised how little they actually ached. Instead, I felt like strength was returning to my abused body. Soon, I would be back in shape enough to be the savior I kept having to be.

My mood instantly darkened at the thought, and I struggled to push away the bitterness. Instead, I focused on the chatter of Ella and Maria as they skipped along. Occasionally, one would break away, running to collect a leaf or rare flower to show me when she returned to grasp my hand.

Overall, the walk was exactly what I needed. When we came upon a huge tree twisted by decades of sea-blown winds, I was properly awed by it. Its thick limbs tangled around each other, white patches of salt build-up showing on its black bark. The spiney, mostly leafless branches stabbed at the sky defiantly, an attitude I could appreciate these days.

"Wow," I said, staring at the stark image.

"Innit cool?" Maria asked. She ran after Ella to circle the trunk, touching it like greeting an old friend.

Both girls jumped up to try to touch the branches just out of reach of even a tall, fully grown man. Then they raced around picking up dried leaves, fallen sticks, and misshapen rocks. Cora moved over to a nearby fallen tree and sat down, appearing content to watch me and the girls.

I filled my eyes with the impressive sight a moment longer, then, glancing at each of my fellow hikers to make sure I was relatively unobserved, I unfocused my eyes, calling up the energy perceiving sight.

The image of the tree immediately switched to black and white, all color draining from the environment for a moment. The colors returned one-by-one, showing me the specific energies of each element as they did.

The tree itself glowed with an aura of deep purple, declaring it strong and important to the rest of the local flora. A speck of yellow shimmered around the branches as an insect inspected the bark for a tasty bite. The grass at the base showed deep greens and browns that were not reflected in their visible color.

I marveled at the interaction of the energies in what seemed like such a barren place. It reminded me that seeing things as dead or useless wasn't always accurate. Sometimes, you had to look at what was going on underneath and inside to see the value.

I turned to look past the tree that ruled this part of the island. I found myself staring at a rocky shoreline. It hadn't occurred to me that we had come so far that we had reached the other side of the island, but it looked like that's what we'd done.

As my gaze moved along the waves rushing in to break against cliffs that stood only a handful of feet over the waterline, I noticed the glowing shapes of animals in the surf. The blue and brown auras surrounded seals leaping over waves and diving around each other.

I smiled at the sight, then caught my breath. There was a woman among them! It seemed odd to have someone so close to the rambunctious creatures, particularly since I couldn't see any sign of scuba gear to keep her from succumbing to the waves and mammalian bodies that periodically jostled her.

I glanced over at Cora and the girls. They hadn't noticed the seals or the woman. I dropped my sight and looked again. The seals were barely visible against the dark water from this distance, and the woman was nowhere to be seen.

I frowned and wondered if I'd just been reading too much into the energies. I shook my head and moved to join Cora, but a movement caught my eye.

CHAPTER 21

My eyebrows raised as the woman approached. She was wearing the brown hide coat again.

"Dr. Roane," I said. "What a nice surprise. I didn't expect to see you again."

The scientist scowled. "A surprise? How is it surprising when you are once again roaming so close to our equipment?"

I leaned back, putting my weight on my heels. It irked me that she was always so aggressive. "Perhaps a sign or two would help us know where we might be infringing. I guess you've just gotten used to bullying the locals into knowing their place."

Dr. Roane flinched. "I didn't say that—"

"Kinda did," I snapped. "Do you have a reason for coming over here, or are you just in the mood to intimidate a couple of kids playing?"

"Nicola!" Cora said, coming up beside me. "Please—"

I held up my hand. "No, I get it," I said. "Don't make waves with the missionaries. Don't make waves with my mother. Don't make waves with the pushy scientists." I turned to face her. "Exactly when do you set any boundaries over who gets to dictate to you in your own home?"

Cora glared at me. "Right now, actually."

I felt a flush move over my face, but I was already dug in. "Why do you let them push you around? Just answer me that. I kind of understand the missionaries, but these researchers need your island, not the other way around."

Cora's face was stony as she replied. "Because it's our choice. Your opinion is the one that not only doesn't matter but is also not asked for."

I glanced at Dr. Roane, half expecting her to be watching with a smug expression. Instead, she seemed confused by Cora's words. Or maybe it was my anger that was throwing her for a loop.

I shook my head and turned to the girls. They were watching with cautious expressions, like they weren't sure what to do. "You girls ready to head back, or was there more?"

Ella sighed and exchanged glances with Maria. "No, Mama. We can go back now."

Her tone was so sad, it broke my heart. It also angered me that they had been so happy until we'd been interrupted. And even though no small part of it was my actions, I glared at Dr. Roane for ruining our expedition.

I took each of the girls' hands and headed back the way we'd come. After a moment, I sighed.

"I'm ready to go back home to Indiana," I said. "How about you?"

The girls shrugged.

"Not missing your beds? Our kitchen? The forest?"

They shrugged again, though there was more hesitation this time.

"You know what I could go for?" I mused aloud. "Pizza from Caboni's, and a slushy. I want brain freeze!"

Ella smiled and Maria hid her mouth behind her free hand.

"What about a movie?" I asked. "A nice dark theater with a big screen and a bucket of popcorn?"

"And chocolates!" Ella blurted out.

Maria nodded. "Or those chewy hot cinnamons."

"Oh, yeah," I exclaimed. "That would be awesome! But what movie would we see?"

Both shouted the name of a recent fairy tale movie, and I groaned. "Oh man! That one is so good!"

They laughed and Ella started singing an overplayed song from the movie. Maria joined in, and I chuckled for a moment before yelling out the chorus.

Movement caught my eye and I saw Cora move up beside us. I stopped singing and let the girls run ahead, enjoying the reminder of our lives. Our real lives, not this pit stop of a vacation turned disaster.

After a moment, I cleared my throat, stealing myself for the hard work of apologizing. "I'm sorry, Cora," I said, keeping my voice low. "You were right. It wasn't my place to decide where you make your stand."

Cora nodded. "You have a lot of passion for what you see as right and wrong. As such, I can appreciate what you were doing. But you tend to run roughshod over people who don't necessarily agree with your perceptions. It's that part that people have a problem with."

I nodded and sighed. "Yeah. I know. I need to work on that." I bit my lip before continuing. "I've just been in a few tough situations lately where I can't take the time to question myself. I didn't have that luxury. And I don't have the practice to fall back on, so I feel insecure, if I'm being honest. That comes out in me just steamrollering. It sucks, but I also don't know how to do better."

I glanced at the young woman. She was intelligent and even wise for her years, but it struck me that I was dumping a lot of stuff on her. I shook my head.

"I shouldn't be putting this on you," I muttered.

Cora shrugged. "It's fine. We have learned a long time ago that sometimes you just need to let it out, and we can listen, even if we aren't really trained to help." She shot me a wry smile. "I could charge you by the hour, if it makes you feel better."

I laughed. "I've already got a therapist on retainer," I said. "Not that I can tell her everything any more than I can tell you everything."

Cora's expression became serious. "You need to tell someone all this stuff you keep to yourself. Isn't there anyone who would understand?"

I shrugged. "A couple of ravens and maybe Joseph, but I can't just call up Joseph right now."

Cora nodded. "And these... ravens, did you say?" Her eyebrow was nearly up to her hairline.

I grinned. "Yup. Ravens." I thought about Huginn and Muninn for a moment. "Maybe I can get a hold of them."

Cora raised her other eyebrow but, to her credit, didn't dismiss my words out of hand. "It might be worth a shot."

I glanced at her. "You don't seem to be too disturbed by the idea that I might confide in birds."

She shrugged. "We believe the fish we eat might come back and demand our life energy in payment. Bird therapists are... not outside the realm of what's possible."

I laughed softly at that, knowing she was at least partially serious. The silence that followed was more companionable, and I was relieved that I hadn't ruined my friendship with the younger woman.

I thought about what she'd said though, and I realized I had been jumping in to save people from themselves and others. The problem was none of them seemed to want to be saved. I was making that decision without respecting their autonomy. Sure, I thought they were wrong to accept being pushed around, but, aside from my girls, it wasn't my place to decide they needed saving.

I heaved a sigh, feeling the strain of our brisk, long walk beginning to wear at my recovering muscles.

I, personally, hated it when someone came in and decided what I did and didn't need. Wasn't that my whole issue with the missionaries pushing salvation upon me and those I cared about?

Sweet baby Baldr, I was effectively proselytizing my own life choices at the indigenous people of the island, pretending I was purer in my intent and methods than those Christians focused on making sure the natives weren't too primitive.

And just like the missionaries, I was working from a place where I believed I knew better. Dammit!

I berated myself a bit longer, then wrestled my thoughts back to the ravens. I had been working alone this whole time, but I knew how to get help. Just like at the Healing Center, I'd gotten caught up in my own issues, believing I needed to deal with everything on my own. Instead, I'd just wallowed in self-pity until I'd made things worse.

I decided that, no matter what, I was visiting the astral plane to find my friends and ask them for help and support. It was either that or fail alone. And failure was a really crappy option, for me and everyone else involved.

CHAPTER 22

I waited until the tiny home was quiet for the night before I went into the astral plane. Like an old friend, it was easy enough to fall back into the rhythm of breathing and the mindset to leave my body.

I opened my mind's eye and found myself in the familiar space of contrasting images. The silver-blue of the Bifrost ribboned across the sky, giving me an anchor in this place. Odd-looking creatures of myth and imagination populated the surreal landscape.

I turned away, refocusing on my task. I called out to my friends and hoped they would hear me. It took several moments of waiting before I decided they weren't going to answer. I called out again, then chewed on my lip, wondering what else to do.

I thought about doing a searching, but lately that had always dumped me into Jehovah's Garden, and I really didn't want to deal with that today. I finally decided to try to find a new way of searching.

Instead of closing my eyes, I let my inner vision unfocus. The shapes and forms that danced around the edges of my sight pulled my attention, but I merely acknowledged the image and let it move away.

I concentrated on the Runespell as I knew it. The general shape and material was easy. All of the Runespells had been a silvery metal about an inch in diameter. The sharp lines of the runes crossed in the center of a circle boundary with a small ring at the top for wearing.

I also knew that the ring was something that only appeared when the user wanted to wear it. Otherwise, the Runespell was just a disk. The size seemed to be somewhat variable, as well, since they were as comfortable holding in the palm as wearing as charms around the neck.

I refocused, recognizing that my thoughts were trailing off. A silvery disk with lines across it. I need to find that.

The weight on my neck seemed to shift, and I frowned. No, not the Runespells I'd already collected. I needed one that wasn't attached to the length of Gleipnir.

Thinking of the chain that bound Fenrir caused my thoughts to return to the cave. I quickly swallowed back the fear and anxiety that memories of facing the wolf-beast and eliminating Bob brought back in a flood.

After breathing deeply for a few moments, my mind cleared enough to safely continue working actively with the astral plane. I let my mind work over the symbols on the Runespells that I was already familiar with. I knew which runes were left, and I considered which might be associated with calming storms.

The angular shapes manifested as red-limned icy blue lines that drew themselves into the air before me. I reached out to trace each as I thought about their names and the interpretations given for rune casting.

I was more into bind runes, the combining of runes for spell work, than rune casting, a form of divination that used runes to see beyond.

The phrase brought a smile to my face. No one ever specified beyond what. Mostly that was because it was hard to explain. It was beyond the present, beyond the physical, beyond the experience of the reader to know, beyond even the knowledge of mankind. Any one of those worked, yet none encompassed the whole of it, and none was encompassed wholly itself. So it was just beyond.

"It's beyond me," I muttered aloud, reveling in the irony for a moment. "Just like this Runespell I need to find."

"Which Runespell?" The raspy voice sounded behind me.

I spun around, nearly losing my footing and drifting away. I let the familiar weight of gravity fill my consciousness for a moment to get my balance.

"Which to seek?" A second, nearly identical voice croaked.

My face broke into a grin. "Huginn! Muninn! You made it!"

The twin ravens bobbed their heads up and down, expressing both agreement and excitement in the movement.

The slightly reddish one stretched its neck upwards, its beak opening wide. "We come."

"You called," the other echoed, its blue-tinted feathers rustling as it shook itself.

I plopped down on the sparse grass in front of them and dropped my chin into my palm. "Am I glad to see you," I said through a jaw locked between the weight of my head and my hand.

"Weren't sure..." Huginn said.

"Welcome we." Muninn finished.

I chewed over their words. They didn't speak plainly, but they made their meaning clear if one paid enough attention. I'd managed to do well in translating during our prior meetings, and I didn't think tripping over communication now would be good for my self-esteem.

"You didn't think you'd be welcome?" At their affirmative caws, I shook my head. "Why would you think that?"

"Independent woman."

"Never ask for help."

"Go it alone."

"Do it for yourself."

I hung my head hearing their back-and-forth response. "I don't ask my friends for help. I'm independent. Perhaps too much so?"

Both ravens turned their heads as if to make sure they weren't looking me in the eye. That body language was loud and clear.

"And I can get defensive about it." I pressed my lips together. "I'm sorry. I know I shouldn't do that. Sometimes I'm just too stubborn."

"Yes," one of the ravens said, though I couldn't tell which. Both of them seemed a bit embarrassed from the outburst.

I laughed. "Yeah. But you'll forgive me, right?"

The ravens cawed assurances and hopped closer to my legs. "Of course, of course!"

I leaned back on both hands, locking my elbows to support my weight. "Glad to hear I'm not persona non grata." I grinned for a moment, then let my expression grow more serious. "So, can you help me?"

"You seek one Runespell..."

"Near to you."

Both ravens finished. "But which one?"

I cocked my head to one side. "I would have thought you'd known about my run-in with Rán."

The birds bobbed enthusiastically. "Yes, yes."

I nodded and waited for them to make the connection. Instead, they simply watched me.

"Uh, she wanted me to find the ninth, to calm storms?" I offered.

"And that's the one..."

"You seek now?"

I frowned in confusion. The god-creatures often spoke in riddles, but they didn't usually just go off the rails about stuff. They had a reason. I gathered my thoughts and tried to figure out how best to get to the core of the communication confusion. "You're talking like there's another Runespell to find. Is there a second Runespell in the area?" A thought struck me, and I added quickly, "Aside from the ones I already wear."

The ravens exchanged a glance.

"We thought you knew..."

"About the other."

"We should not have brought it up..."

"If you didn't know."

"We can say no more."

I sighed in disappointment but nodded. "I understand. Thank you for giving me that much." I sat enjoying their company for a long moment, watching the symbolic waves nearby.

The ravens soon came closer, Muninn pecking at my pants to get my attention. "You are sad."

I nodded. "I'm tired." The birds cocked their heads toward each other, bringing a smile to my face. "I don't know. Since the thing in the cave..." I trailed off.

"With the wolf?" Huginn asked.

"Yeah," I mumbled. "And Bob. It just took something out of me. I mean, everything I've done has taken something out of me, but I can't seem to get it back this time."

"That is why..."

"You took this trip?"

I sighed. "Yeah. It was supposed to be relaxing. I think I relaxed right out of being a berserker, though."

The ravens cocked their heads the other way, perfectly synchronized.

"You can't berserk?"

"Rade fixed that."

I grimaced. "She fixed it for a while. But, ever since the shipwreck..."

The birds watched me closely.

I ignored them, sitting up suddenly. I grasped the pendants at my neck and one of them grew cold as I reviewed the Runespells through the knowledge of Odin from the fourteenth Runespell. "An eighth I know..."

I caught the raven's exchange of glances. "Am I right?" I demanded. "Is the eighth in play?"

The birds hopped around, acting nervous.

"We don't know which..."

"For certain, but..."

"That would be one..."

"That it could be."

They paused their back-and-forth chant, then spoke together. "It is likely."

I nodded. "Good enough. The eighth. Dammit, that would explain so much. Calming a warrior spirit. Using it on me, though? That implies someone with a pretty close knowledge of who I am and what I am doing here." I considered for a moment. "Either the person using the ninth is also using the eighth, or someone is protecting them."

The ravens exchanged another look, but I ignored them, getting the idea in my teeth and running with the possibilities. "It would be just like Jehovah to have his minions do something like this. Damn him!" I chewed on my lower lip for a moment. "Let's see. I lost it in the community center one, two, three... maybe four times? That's got to be where I have encountered the person. That means it could be... well, crap. Pretty much anyone, still."

The ravens bobbed in synch. "Careful, though."

"Assumptions made."

"Good to start."

"Confirm first."

I sat back, nodding. "You're right. I am jumping in with both feet before I know any facts. I have some ideas, though, and that's more than I had before." I smiled at my friends. "Ideas and some support from those who care."

Huginn flipped its beak up and opened it in a birdie smile. "Careful."

Muninn mirrored the action. "Assumptions."

I paused and looked at them. "What am I assuming now?"

"That no one with you..."

"In your exile..."

"Cares." Both birds finished together.

I pressed my lips together. "I know you're right, but it really feels like I've been flapping in the wind with this one."

"This is different?"

"Then times before?"

I sighed. "Guess not. And I'm usually pleasantly surprised how much support I actually end up having." I let my head drop. "I'm not very good at seeing my allies, am I?"

The birds crowded close to me as they spoke as one. "No one ever is."

CHAPTER 23

After Huginn and Muninn spent several more minutes telling me funny stories about their recent travels, I left them. I felt guilty letting them assume I was going back to my body, but I didn't want to think too much about the pit stop I was making first.

I closed my eyes on their black feathered faces and focused, waiting for the world to shift jarringly around me.

"Can I get no peace from you?"

I opened my eyes to face the old man form that represented my adversary. "Hey, Jehovah. No peace for the wicked, ya know." I watched him bristle at the implication.

"What do you want now?" he intoned, a thread of annoyance coloring his words. He shifted, tucking his hands deeper into his sleeves, and his chin raised a fraction.

I stifled a smile. A god was discombobulated by little ol' me. Excellent. "I was wondering why you gave your minions two Runespells this time."

"Two?" Jehovah snapped his mouth shut on the word and stared at me stonily.

I narrowed my eyes at him. "Did you give the missionaries a Runespell?"

Jehovah pressed his lips together and stared at a spot over my left shoulder.

I ground my jaw and pulled out my ace. "I ask you for a third time." The god's eyes widened in shock. Gods and god-creatures could seldom refuse to truthfully answer a thrice-asked question. I was stretching it a bit to include the question from the previous encounter, but it was the same question and would therefore count. "Did you give the missionaries any of the Runespells, directly or indirectly?"

The god narrowed his eyes at me. "No. Now, leave."

I gasped as the world tilted and I was flung backwards. I closed my eyes against the spinning visuals and struggled to recenter myself. After a long, gut-churning moment, I was able to tug myself back into my body.

I lay on my back for a long time, staring at the ceiling and thinking over the information I'd gotten. On the one hand, I felt better knowing that my friends were still there, waiting to help me. And it wasn't my fault or weakness that had caused my berserker to keep failing.

I ground my teeth at that, but I breathed steadily until I could let the anger go. It wouldn't do me any good to be upset about it now, in the middle of the night.

Instead, I thought about the shock of Jehovah's answer. I'd been absolutely certain that he'd gotten one of the Runespells into the hands of one missionary or another. I worried that my phrasing of the question had been the problem, and I reviewed my words over and over.

When the little wall clock showed 3:30 am, I sighed. I needed to get some sleep if I was going to function in the morning. And I needed to function if I was going to figure all of this out in the next few days.

I rolled over, finding the comfiest position, and let myself drift off.

• • •

"Nicola, are you ready?"

I blinked, staring at Julie in confusion. Then I remembered I was supposed to meet with her and my mother.

"Oh, yeah. Okay." I followed her into the office and sat in the chair next to Mom. I ignored the look my mom gave me as the missionary woman-slash-counselor took her seat behind the desk.

"Last time, we were talking about how you felt you'd been through more than your mother could understand. Right, Nicola?"

I nodded. I could see my mom watching me from the corner of my eye.

"You still feel that way?"

"I guess," I said. "Look, can we do this another time? I have something important to get done."

Both women stared at me.

"More important than your relationship with your mother?" Julie asked. "Marylou, how does Nicola saying that make you feel?"

Mom sniffed. "It's pretty much what I've come to expect from her—"

I sat forward. "So, we are just going to pretend I don't have somewhere I need to be?"

Julie narrowed her eyes at me. "We are going to pretend you care about your mother's feelings at all." She turned back to my mother. "You were saying?"

"She acts like whatever she's doing is life or death. Like her responsibilities are so important. Like she's saving the world or something."

I slouched down in my chair, the weight of the irony becoming too much. "Or something," I muttered.

Julie turned to me. "Do you have something to add?"

I grimaced. "You wouldn't believe me if I told you. And I'm a bad daughter either way, so, yeah. I am saving the world. What I'm doing is life or death. Sorry I didn't tell you that before." I rolled my eyes at the two of them. "Even more, though, I'm sorry I can't prove it to you. I can't give you any evidence that I have this huge important thing and I'm not just being mean to you."

Mom frowned at me. "That's just not a realistic excuse, Nicola."

I shrugged. "It's the truth, so it's the only one you're getting from me." I scowled at Julie. "Contrary to what you both seem to think of me, I'm not a liar."

Julie shook her head. "Does feeling like you have the weight of the world on your shoulders make it okay for you to treat people badly?"

"Is having that kind of responsibility the only thing that would give me the right to set a boundary?" I shot back.

"What boundaries do you think you are setting?" Julie asked.

I cracked my neck, doing my best to ignore the patronizing tone in her question. "Firstly, that it is my right to believe in my religion." I held up a finger and lifted a second as I continued. "Secondly, that it is my right to teach my kids what I believe. Thirdly, that it isn't fair to act like those rights impede on you."

"Taking the kids to church isn't a bad thing," my mother said.

I raised my eyebrows. "Funny how that only works when it's you and your church, though. You questioned me for weeks when I took the girls to that event in Indianapolis."

Julie looked at my mom questioningly.

Mom shrugged. "There were Satanists there. I was worried for them."

Julie looked back at me, eyebrows high on her forehead.

I sighed. "It was a multi-traditional event. Lots of beliefs were represented. You just assumed I either wasn't paying attention to the girls or had trotted them right up to a Satanic altar for sacrifice."

I cocked my head to the side to shoot her a tight smile. "Mind you, I knew those particular Satanists, and they are parents themselves, and sweethearts besides. You have so much bias against certain religions, you never bothered asking about the people themselves."

Mom looked at Julie. "Do you see? I'm supposed to give actual Satanists a pass for influencing my granddaughters just because she says they are okay."

I rolled my eyes. "Yeah. That's 'cause I'm their mother. I'm the one who has to determine these things."

Julie looked from Mom to me. "And you think your judgment is that sound?"

I felt my eyebrows shoot up. "Excuse you?"

She shrugged. "You took your daughters to see Satanists. That's not very good judgment."

I shook my head. "This is why I need to set that boundary. You both are so judge-y and hateful..."

I stood up, ready to leave. I could feel the cougar inside me coiled up and ready to pounce. It was a good feeling, like I still had some kind of power left over my life.

As I stood, my mother flinched and Julie frowned. I shot angry looks at both of them, keeping my anger leashed, but letting it sit in my gut. I turned on my heel to leave.

The world kept spinning and my head felt like it was floating away. My eyes wouldn't focus and my knees gave out. I fell, barely catching myself on the chair I'd just vacated.

I heard Julie speaking to my mother. "I think we're done here. I'm sorry I couldn't do more to help."

Mom muttered something that seemed to satisfy the woman and Julie left. I watched her walk out without any way to stop and question her. Had she been the cause of this weakness? Was she using the eighth Runespell?

After a moment, the sudden weakness ebbed, and I could manage arms and legs in a semblance of coordination. I grumbled and muttered to myself as I worked on getting back on my feet. My mother helped me up after a moment, her expression accusatory.

"What?" I asked.

"What is right," she said. "You are... all over the place. What is wrong with you?"

I stared out the door after Julie, wondering if I had the strength to catch up to her. "I can't tell you," I muttered.

CHAPTER 24

Once I got my strength back enough to follow, I hurried from the office. Julie was nowhere to be seen. I asked one of the locals if they'd seen her, and she had apparently gone back to the missionary camp for the day. I took a deep breath. I could follow her, or I could focus on the other Runespell for the time being.

Jehovah's words came back to me, and I chewed my lip, wondering how he'd managed to loophole my question. Maybe he answered for the "one Runespell" being the ninth, the one controlling storms, instead of the eighth, the one calming warrior spirits.

Or he might be one of the few gods who could, by nature, lie. There were so few of those, it was hardly worth exploring, but...

One of the pendants against my chest went icy-cold and I knew that Jehovah was not one of the gods who could lie. I spared a second of gratitude for the fourteenth Runespell's knowledge, but I also felt a tendril of disappointment. That would have tied my dilemma up nicely.

Perhaps he hadn't considered Julie to be a missionary, since she was functioning as a counselor for me and a few others. In that case, her job description would allow her to slip through the verbal cracks.

I nodded to myself and decided a trip to the missionary's camp was next on the list. I turned to head out and nearly ran Catherine over in my haste.

"Oh, I'm so sorry!" I squawked.

Catherine smiled and patted my arm. "It's fine, Nicola. Where are you headed in such a hurry?"

I felt my cheeks go hot. "Um, well."

The older woman watched me with a neutral expression, but I knew I wouldn't be able to get away with hedging or lying.

I swallowed. "I was going to find Julie. She went back to the camp."

Catherine sighed. "Really? And why?"

"I just need to ask her some questions," I said. "I think she might have something more to do with... something that's going on with me and my mother. You know, something other than just her playing counselor."

Catherine shook her head. "Are you sure that's all?"

I shrugged. "If I'm right, she might know something else that I need to know. It seems to be all connected. The storms, the Yup'ik, the missionaries, even the ship sinking..."

I let my words trail off as I caught the disbelieving look on the woman's face.

"Do you honestly think the missionaries had something to do with your shipwreck?" she asked. "Did they cause the storm, then?"

I shook my head, looking down at my feet. "No. That was Rán."

Catherine raised her eyebrows. "Another one of your gods?"

I nodded. "She wants me to find someone who is stopping the storms."

She blinked several times, surprise flashing momentarily across her face. "Why would a Norse god want to interfere with an alignalghi?"

It was my turn to blink. I'd forgotten about the Yup'ik spiritual intermediaries. As I recalled, they were known to convince spirits to calm storms. I shook my head. "No, no. Same concept, different process."

"Oh," Catherine said. "Very well. So you believe someone is using a different... process? To calm storms? And that angers this Rán?"

I nodded. "Yeah. And the missionaries keep coming in with these flood and storm stories, like storms are punishment but their god will stop them. If they are doing it, they might attribute it to a miracle to help them guide the Yup'ik to their beliefs."

Catherine shook her head. "You really need to stop with that, Nicola."

I frowned. "Stop with what? I just want to help."

Catherine stared at me. "I know," she said. "But you are 500 years too late for that. We already lost. Over and over again, we've lost."

She looked over at the other locals scattered throughout the community center. My eyes followed her gaze. I saw the people passively, patiently, waiting for the next thing to happen.

"Have you ever known what it's like to be in a battle that you can't win?" Sorrow filled her eyes. "We know we aren't going to make it. All we can do is make some kind of statement as we go out."

I nodded. "Yeah, I get that one."

She glanced at me, doubt written on her face. Something in my expression must have convinced her I might know what I was talking about, though, because her features relaxed after a moment.

"We can only make that statement if we do it ourselves," she said softly. "No qat'sqaq can save us. If you try, you will take away the only thing we have left – hope that our dying voices will cut the ice from your people's hearts."

My head dropped to hide the burning tears that leaked from my eyes. "It's not fair," I muttered. "Every other time I've gone after Runespells, I was able to save the people involved, somehow."

Catherine patted my shoulder. "Tell me, Taquka'aq arnaq. Why are you here?"

I took a deep breath and lifted my face, raising my chin a bit in an attempt to retain my pride. "I am here to find and collect pendants that hold powers that are unsafe in the hands they are in."

Catherine raised her eyebrows. "Well, aren't you the gallant knight." She leaned forward and whispered to me. "Stick to your quest, knight. Not every damsel in distress is yours to save." She turned back to watch her people milling around once again. "We are not your quest. Stop acting like you get to save us."

"Get to?" I laughed. "I don't think you understand how hard saving people is."

Catherine locked her eyes on mine. Her slow smile was sad, and it filled me with dread for what she was going to say. "I understand. I also understand that, no matter how hard the saving is, it's easier to live with than watching the slow death of an entire people. And that's the part you are afraid of. I know. It's the part I'm afraid of too."

I bit my lip. After several moments, I nodded. "You're right," I whispered. "I'm more afraid of not saving people than I am of the dangers involved in putting myself at risk."

"Yup." Catherine heaved a sigh. "But you, Taquka'aq arnaq, have your own path to walk. It is no less difficult or important than the slow erosion of my culture, my people."

"Why do you keep calling me that?" I asked. "Taquka'aq arnaq? What does that mean?"

Catherine shrugged. "It means 'bear woman'. I call you that because that is what you are."

I frowned. "Norse berserkers were thought to have the spirit of a bear," I said.

"Exactly."

I shook my head. "Not exactly. My spirit is a mountain lion."

Catherine considered this for a moment. "Figures," she said. "A qat'sqaq always has to do things a little different."

I laughed. "It's because we are really focused on the whole 'rugged individualism' thing."

The older woman snorted. "People aren't meant to be individuals unless they are being sacrificed."

I sighed. "Well, that would apply, too."

Catherine shook her head. "Look, if you still need to go after the missionaries, that's your quest. Just make sure you aren't doing it to save us. Focus on what your goal is. Don't get distracted by other people's problems. We forgive you for not saving us."

The earnest expression on her face was almost too much for me. I nodded and turned away. Then I stopped and turned back to her. "Thank you."

Without looking back again, I headed out the door to find my target.

CHAPTER 25

It took me nearly half an hour to hike across the space between the village and the missionary's camp. It was obviously a well-used spot, as there was a path worn among the trees and brush on the way.

I tried to plan out what to say, but I was drawing a blank. How was I going to accuse the woman of using a magical pendant to weaken me without sounding accusing? Or of making her think I was saying she was using witchcraft. That kind of buzzword stuff would have her bristling and unhelpful in a heartbeat.

That was if she was going to be helpful at all in the first place. Given how things had gone down at the counselling session, I wasn't sure she'd even see me.

As I moved through the brush along the path, I realized how loud I was. It was the kind of thing that wouldn't have bothered me years ago, but it really bugged me since the mountain lion spirit had taken up residence. My lack of grace was an insult to the big cat.

I focused on that annoyance and pulled at the spirit inside me. After a few moments of concentration and focus on my footsteps, I'd achieved near silence in my movement. I let myself feel a touch of pride, pushing aside the inner voice that sneered at me about how long it had taken for me to reach this stage.

I strode into the worn clearing filled with high-tech tents and pavilions. Camp chairs, folding tables and a few camp kitchens interspersed throughout. People moved around, picking up, cleaning up, or just chatting with each other.

I looked around for Julie, spotting her at one of the camp kitchens, stirring a large stock pot over a gas flame cooktop. She didn't notice me until I walked up to her, then she started, as if she was a bit frightened.

"Hey, Julie," I said, keeping my voice low and soft. "I-uh, I just wanted to apologize."

She waited, stirring the pot, but I could tell her focus was on me.

I cleared my throat. "Um, well. I shouldn't have said the things that I said."

"Which things were those?" she asked.

I pressed my lips together. I was familiar with this passive-aggressive game. "I shouldn't blame you and my mother for not understanding."

Julie looked up. "No, you shouldn't. Nor should you attack us for trying to help you. Nicola, you are very lost." She shook her head.

I took a deep breath. "I have been going the wrong way about a lot of things since... well, since the shipwreck, but also before that."

"I'm aware," she said. "Marylou told me how you have been moving farther from the church, putting your faith in shrinks who let you use these false gods as reasons for your blasphemy."

I pressed my lips together. This wasn't going to be easy, keeping my temper while trying to weed out information with this level of hostility. "I see—"

"I don't think you do," Julie snapped. "Your mother is a good Christian woman, and you cause her nothing but pain and heartache. You should obey your mother, not cause her problems."

I felt the muscles in my forehead aching as my brows drew tighter and tighter into a scowl. "So you condone abuse."

Her eyes went wide. "Of course not—"

"But you are." I didn't let her get her response out. "I try very hard to give her, and you, the benefit of the doubt. However, she won't let me be the parent to my kids. She disrespects their mother and uses the fact that she is my mother to do so."

Julie frowned and opened her mouth, but I pushed on.

"In addition, you both act like I'm somehow so ignorant that the problem is that I just don't know enough about Christianity to believe. I know. I believe in your god. I just think he's a dick."

Her eyes went wide and anger flashed in them. I cut her off again.

"Don't think for one minute I don't know what you are doing. You have this idea that I need to be shown a better way or something." My voice grew louder and Julie began to shrink back. "But you need to accept that I simply don't agree with you!"

My words ended on a shout, and Julie flinched away from them like they had been a blow. She slipped on the packed grasses and fell to the ground.

A shout from behind me had me turning around, my vision washing yellow. I embraced the anger and the berserker power, feeling strong and in control for the first time in weeks. Months, even.

Several of the men had come up, looking ready for anything, which struck me a particularly non-Christian. What happened to turning the other cheek?

One man slipped around me and reached out to help Julie stand up. Another moved to grab my arm, and I pulled it away.

"Don't touch me," I roared.

Two more men flanked me and the three of them moved in to grapple me. Part of me raged that they didn't even try to engage me with words. They were going to use their masculine bulk to force me to do what they decided was right.

The yellow completely took over the color palate of my sight. I shrank in on myself and waited for them to surround me, closing in, clawing at my arms and clothes.

With a roar of fury, I flung my arms out and sprang up. The berserker-enhanced jump sent me flying over their heads in a backflip that, a decade ago, I couldn't have even imagined myself pulling off.

I landed on my feet behind the group, crouching down and snarling. Several of the missionaries reached for the crosses around their necks. My eyes flickered to Julie, who also reached for the chain on her neck.

I glared at her, waiting for the weakness to flood my body. Instead, she pulled out a small silver cross and moved her mouth as if praying.

I scowled, turning over that information in my mind. The men were edging toward me again, but I judged that I still had a double handful of seconds before I needed to act and ignored them.

With the display of anger I'd just made, Julie should have been all over using the eighth Runespell to knock me down. But she hadn't. I searched over and over for another explanation, but I had to finally admit that the problem was that Julie didn't have the Runespell.

Someone else had been using it on me.

I stood upright suddenly, and the men flinched back. Ignoring them in favor of the thoughts running circles in my head, I turned on my heel and strode away from the camp.

There hadn't been many others who had been present or even nearby when the weakness had overtaken me. My mother would have been my first suspect, but where would she have gotten it from? She'd been with me and the girls for a week before the shipwreck, then she'd been a stranger on the island for only a few days before I'd started feeling the sudden bouts of weakness.

I shook my head and began reviewing the faces I could recall from each of my visits to the community center. Elizabeth's face came to mind, and I pressed my lips together. There was no reason I could see for the young woman to have done such a thing to me.

Except I was only guessing that it had only been used on me. There were plenty of people who had exhaustion or fatigue from long winters, the shipwreck, or even just age. But what if it had been something else that was affecting them?

I lengthened my stride and headed back to the community center.

CHAPTER 26

I entered the community center with a purpose that spilled out of me in waves. Several people glanced at me when I stepped through the door, then backed away when their eyes landed on my face. Others didn't look at me but edged away as if sensing the intensity of my focus.

I immediately shifted my vision to view the energies around me. Though I couldn't see my own energy, the effects of it rippled the auras of the people around me. The room was filled with color, dimmed by a dull patina of politeness that coated most of the energies.

A quick check told me that most of the pops of clear, passionate colors were from the children running throughout, playing tag, or inventing some other game with whatever was on hand. Instead, I focused on the sharp spines that were not attached to kids.

I dismissed the ruddy rose of loving and sexual passion. That couple was too far involved in each other to have been worried about what I was or wasn't doing. Instead, I looked for strong colors from people who were watching me or others, likely with the energy of fear or anger. Those kinds of emotions would drive one to suppress another.

I stalked through the center looking for both the energy, and Elizabeth's face. After a moment, I realized I must have been glaring, because even those people I knew enough to be friendly with were shrinking back from me. I shook my head and decided it was time to get answers and get out before the tension in the air snapped in an unexpected way.

I spotted a local villager who I'd seen speaking to Cora on several occasions. I walked up to her and tried not to sniff satisfactorily at the extra tendril of fear that wove through her energy.

"Do you know where I can find Elizabeth?" I ground out. At the woman's hesitation, I made my face relax a bit and tried to reassure her. "I just need to ask her some questions. Very important questions."

"She went to the research station," the woman croaked. "She's making a delivery."

I nodded and turned on my heel. Several people caught my eye at that point. Their energy was the flavor of someone who'd gotten up the courage to do the right thing, at least in their own mind. And it was directed at me.

I smiled as my vision washed a bit more yellow in preparation for whatever they were about to do. One of them stepped forward and my eyes locked on him, focusing on a spot just in front of his chest so my peripheral vision would catch any movement he made. Because I didn't look at his face, I didn't realize who it was until he spoke.

"Nicola," Jeremiah said soothingly. "Let us help you."

I cocked my head to one side, but I didn't respond. I didn't need his help, and he wasn't really offering. The comment was just bait to draw my attention and energy into a conversation that he would control.

His jaw worked for a moment as he realized I wasn't going to engage with him. "We can help you, you know," he said, his voice low and calm. He sounded like he was trying to sooth a flighty horse.

I ran my tongue over my teeth. I definitely wasn't a horse, and he wasn't going to be soothing me. I glanced around once more, looking for any hints that there was something else here that I needed to pay attention to.

Suddenly, I noticed my mother's frown in the back of the crowd. She caught me looking at her and she ducked her head, covering her study of me by pretending to search through her purse.

I shook my head. It was ridiculous how often she passed judgment but, the moment she had a chance to really confront me, she backed off. I glanced around again and strode toward the door walking straight at the preacher rather than moving around him.

He tried to stare me down as I approached, but I barely noticed. At the last moment, he jumped out of the way, and I moved out the door without a backwards glance.

The research station.

I focused on that moving quickly out of the village and along the faint pathway that I'd walked with the girls and Cora only a few days before. I wondered for a moment how Dr. Roane would react to my very obvious intrusion after she'd been so hostile about our accidental trespassing.

A smile quirked my lips and I kept walking, my mind turning over possible scenarios with the doctor and with Elizabeth. I tried to pull myself away from any thoughts that got too aggressive. I was riding the mountain lion spirit hard today, and enough of me recognized that to realize the danger inherent in doing so.

As it turned out, I didn't get far past the small sign delineating the grounds of the research station and its extraneous buildings. Instead, I found Elizabeth walking toward me, pulling a large, wheeled camp wagon and talking to a group of women, all wearing the odd suede coats.

I stopped a few yards away and let the others make up the distance. They fell silent as they got close and stopped several feet away. The scientists milled around, as if nervous. The predator in me was pleased by their unconscious fear.

Elizabeth wasn't afraid. She narrowed her eyes at me. "What are you doing here?" she demanded. "Bothering Dr. Roane again?"

My eyes flicked over to the doctor's face, and my mouth twitched with the smile I strove to hide. "Dr, Roane is of no consequence to me," I said. "I am here to talk to you."

Elizabeth seemed taken aback by my words. She raised an eyebrow and frowned. "Okay. Talk."

I took a deep breath, considering how to approach the topic. I stood with my feet slightly spread for maximum balance, and I had my arms crossed. I knew the pose was intimidating, and I decided to use that to my advantage. "You've been trying to control people," I accused her.

"Excuse you?" Elizabeth's frown turned into a scowl. "How would I control people? And who would I be controlling?"

I watched her face, letting the silence draw out before I spoke. I let my voice draw out the words in the kind of pseudo-casual drawl that spoke of violence. "Me, for one," I said. "And you have... something. A pendant or a sigil of some kind. Maybe you found it, or maybe someone gave it to you."

Elizabeth's face reflected anger at the accusation, but also confusion. Doubt crept into my mind.

"Silver in color," I pressed. My eyes began moving to the other faces in the small group. "Did you touch it, or was it set into something larger?"

Elizabeth shook her head. "I have no idea what you are talking about. You've got some nerve, though, making that kind of accusation. Why would I want to control anyone?"

I frowned. "Are you telling me that you don't... want people to calm down and then they just... do?"

"How would I do that?" she demanded. She glanced around at the women surrounding her as if asking for support. "What? Are the natives supposed to be all mystical and ooooh? You think the primitives still play with spirits and are after your precious qat'sqaq will?"

I scowled and snorted. "Oh, please. Save me from your victim card and prideful disdain of your own history."

Elizabeth's eyes went wide and she opened her mouth, but I cut her off.

"Oh, I get it. Your people have been oppressed and marginalized. I get that, and I respect that to the best of my limited understanding of your situation." My eyes narrowed. "But I won't let you weaponize it so you can bludgeon me with your victimhood. I asked you a question in all honesty. You can at least address it with the same."

Elizabeth flushed a deep red and dropped her eyes, but she didn't argue my point. After a moment of pressing her lips together, she answered, "No. That doesn't happen. I don't know how it could."

I sighed, reading her energy and seeing only honesty in her response. My gaze flicked to the group of scientists. I chewed my lower lip as I watched them, considering.

Dr. Roane stepped forward. "Elizabeth, thank you for delivering those items. We look forward to seeing you again next week."

Elizabeth looked at her in surprise but, after a moment's hesitation, simply walked toward the village with the cart. Dr. Roane watched her until she was well out of hearing range, then turned to face me.

She stared at me for a long moment. "You speak of the Runespells, don't you? This changes much about what we thought of your previous behavior."

I nodded, my eyes narrowing.

The doctor held up a hand when I opened my mouth to ask her about her knowledge. "I won't tell you how we know about them. But rest assured. Neither I nor my sisters have or are using any of the Runespells. That magic is not for us to toy with."

I frowned at her phrasing. It was oddly formal, similar to how Mercy and the ravens spoke at times. "Very well," I said. "Do you know who might?"

Dr. Roane frowned. "We could guess, the same as you are doing. But we do not know."

I nodded. "Good enough."

I turned on my heel, lifting my hand to wave at them as I left without another word. On the one hand, I was glad to have eliminated so many possibilities. However, I was still without a clue as to who might have either of the Runespells in play.

I grumbled to myself, and the energy that had buoyed me up all day slipped away.

CHAPTER 27

The next day, I stepped out to find that the village had exploded into action. People ran about with more purpose than I'd seen on the island since I'd gotten here. I flagged down a young man I recognized.

"Samuel," I called. "What's going on?"

The teen barely slowed down, calling over his shoulder. "Supply ship! For the missionaries!" He took several jumping side steps as he finished. "There's gonna be a festival tonight!"

I blinked. "A festival?"

But Samuel had already rushed away. I shook my head at his exuberance and made my way to the community center, figuring I'd be able to find out more there. People rushed around, mostly in the large kitchen, cooking up more food than I'd seen on the island before.

I stopped one of the older women. "What's this for?" I asked, keeping my voice respectful but curious.

"The missionaries like to have a festival while they are here," she said. "They call it a revival, but it's a festival. They bring in lots of food and we—"

"We pretend to like the religious events they put on," finished a voice behind me.

I turned to find Catherine grinning behind me. "That's blasphemy," I pointed out.

"Yes," she admitted, her voice cheerful. "Now, help us get this bread made."

I decided I wasn't going to get much done just running around, so I allowed Catherine to pull me into the kitchen. I spent several hours meditatively shaping loaves, putting them in the hot oven and pulling them out when they turned a lovely, dark golden brown. The ritualistic sequence and delicious smells let my mind relax.

When we finally pulled out the last loaf, one of the older women brandished a knife at me. "We better make sure we didn't mess it up," she said, handing me the knife and pulling out a stick of butter and a spreader.

I grinned and quickly sliced the bread into relatively even, thick slices and passed them to her to slather with butter. Each of the kitchen workers got a slice of the still-warm bread, and the building filled with the sounds of appreciation and smacking lips. Soon, the soups and stews were done and packed up for the festival.

The women had opened up quickly once they saw me working hard alongside them. I learned that the festival was annoying to most of the elders and adults, but everyone got lots of good food, and most of the village elders snuck in a few brews despite the missionaries' teetotaler stance. I learned that the adults found a lot of the events childish and patronizing but safe, so they could relax while the games and plays entertained small children. And I learned that the festival was often held a few days before the missionaries left.

I joked and laughed with the women as we hauled the goods to a relatively flat open space along the beach. It was a good trek away, nearly halfway around the island, but I had to admit it was a perfect spot for the village and missionaries to gather, spread out, and have a good time.

As the sun began lowering in the late afternoon sky, music played and bowls of food were filled and passed around. There were a few plays and sermons going on throughout, but I also spotted several groups that avoided the missionaries.

It only took me a few minutes to find the girls, running around with some of the village children. I glanced around to find my mother nearby, keeping an eye on them. I nodded to her but didn't try to start a conversation. I knew anything we might talk about would just devolve into a fight anyways.

Instead, I let the girls pull me from place to place, talking to people we'd befriended over the last weeks, gulping down helpings of soup and bread, and playing the silly little games with candy and pamphlets for prizes. They never stopped talking, telling me stories I'd heard dozens of times, as well as new adventures they'd had only that morning.

When the sun hung low in the sky, threatening to sink below the horizon, the science team from the research station showed up. They stayed in a group and the missionaries seemed to unconsciously avoid them, but several of the villagers greeted them, drawing them into the celebration.

After several hours, I felt my energy waning. I found a spot on a bench and sat, letting my mind relax and watching the people interact. I got back up to help light a few small fires, using the seventh Runespell to subtly push the flames into the wood when the wind gusted too much.

The woman who had provided the lighter had vanished, so I pocketed the small plastic tube before sitting to enjoy the results of my efforts. The small hearths were scattered around, providing patches of light around which groups gathered, sitting or standing in loose circles.

Some people stayed in place, letting others come to them to talk. Others moved between groups, shifting constantly. Laughter broke out every few minutes as someone told a funny story or joked with friends. Once in a while, voices raised as friendly arguments became passionate, or old debates were revisited.

A few times, a small group of teens tried to sneak away, only to be stopped by a vocal adult who knew what trouble they were going to get into. Other times, I spotted a few younger people successfully leaving the firelit areas.

I smiled over the whole thing, enjoying the people-watching while the girls played quietly nearby. As the last of the light from the setting sun faded from the sky, the moon peeked over the horizon.

I watched as it rose, glad to see it was only a light orange color. Nowhere close to blood red. Tension I hadn't realized I'd been holding in my shoulders faded away and I slumped on the bench.

Catherine sat down beside me while I was staring at the yellow-orange flames of the nearest fire. The girls had been given a blanket and were huddled together in a bundle of limbs and fabric, dozing and murmuring in waves as their energy ebbed away.

We all sat in silence for several minutes before Catherine spoke softly. She pointed out into the ocean where the horizon sparked with flashes of lightning.

"Storm's coming," she said.

I nodded. "Is it going to hit us?"

She shrugged. "Hard to say at this point."

My mother walked up at that moment. "Did you see the storm?" I nodded as she glanced down at the two girls wrapped up in the blanket. "Shouldn't we get back?"

I shrugged as Catherine responded. "It might yet miss us."

Mom glanced worriedly at the sky, then sat on the other side of Catherine, frowning as she watched the crowd mill around. Several people had noticed the lightning, but no one seemed concerned yet. Finally, she sat back and relaxed as the quiet of the late-night celebration washed over us.

I sat with my chin propped up in my hand, trying not to doze off after the full day of work. Conversations had grown softer and the fires had died down to small flames and embers that warmed several feet around them.

I blinked rapidly when I realized I'd dozed off completely. Catherine had shifted next to me, and I followed her gaze to see Cora rushing toward us.

"The storm will hit in about half an hour," she said loudly enough that others could hear her. "I've already got Grandmama home and tucked in safely. We should help pack up and get the kids to shelter."

I nodded and yawned, standing and helping first Catherine, then my mother to their feet. I turned to find Cora gathering up the various carts and wagons that the village had collected for transporting food and tables. Groups of people were quickly breaking down the serving tables, putting lids on pots and wrapping up leftover bread loaves.

I glanced down at the girls, half wishing I could commandeer a large wagon to transport them. They were too heavy to carry, so I knelt down to gently shake them awake. I heard my mother protesting, but she didn't carry on with it long, so she must have realized it was the best option.

Ella sat up with a groggy expression, while Maria shot upright suddenly. I calmed Maria down, talking softly to both of them. "There's a storm coming," I told them. "We need to go back to the village before it starts raining. We don't want to get all cold and wet, do we? That's right, we need to get up. No, no, Ella, we aren't going back to sleep. We need to stand up. That's right, Maria, on your feet."

I droned on, keeping the words coming so they could latch on to them as they fought sleep to wake up enough to walk back. It was a long walk as it was, and I was sure they would be fine once they got moving. I kept one eye on the lightning getting closer and closer.

"Ok," I said, finally getting both girls to their feet and conscious enough to respond to my words. "Let's wrap you up so if it starts raining, you won't be quite as cold." I bundled the blanket around their shoulders as I spoke.

I looked up to find my mother staring at the storm. "Mom? You ready? Did Catherine already leave?"

Mom shook her head. "That strange old woman? She just stood there, staring at the storm, then she went that way." She pointed to the beach toward the storm and away from the village. "She was muttering under her breath." Mom looked at me with a disdainful expression. "Is she crazy?"

I frowned in the direction my mother had pointed. "No, Mom, she's not." I couldn't see anyone in the darkness beyond the fires, but I also wasn't sure if anyone else had seen Catherine leave. The older woman might have trouble getting back if she waited until too close to the storm hitting.

I glanced down at the girls and my mother. "Have you got them, Mom? I'm going to make sure Catherine is okay. I'll catch up in a minute."

The girls blinked up at me, and Mom nodded, tight lipped but without comment. She never did approve of me putting myself out there for other people's benefit. Especially for people who weren't close family. I hugged the girls and trotted in the direction of the beach.

CHAPTER 28

A few times, I stopped and asked people if they'd seen Catherine pass by. No one had. They all got worried looks that turned to relief when I said I'd find her, so I was confident I was making the right choice.

Because of my questions, no one tried to wrangle me into packing up the foods and tables. Those not directly involved in the conversations simply nodded as I passed.

Within a few moments, I'd left the remaining crowd and made my way into the darkness. I blinked several times to get my eyes used to the lack of light. Normally, the stars or bright moonlight would ease the transition. But with the storm clouds covering the night sky, there was no source of light beyond the low fires except for the sporadic flashes of lightning.

As I made my way carefully through the slight brush around the beach, the sound of voices faded into the white noise of waves crashing. The sound was irregular and seemed to surround the noise of birds and distant thunder.

I nearly tripped over a bush that was half hidden in the extra darkness of a slope, then staggered as the earth dropped from under my feet. I ran in a jerky motion, trying to find the steeply-sloped gravel with my feet.

I nearly made it, finally getting the feel of the decline, then it levelled out and I stepped too hard, aiming for inches below the ground. The jarring effect of missing the steps sent me tumbling to one knee and both hands.

I bit down on the squawk that raced up my throat. Instead, I simply froze, taking deep breaths to calm my racing heart. I reached for the berserker, not wanting the rage but needing the better night vision.

Yellow washed over the blue-black of the night, lending the shapes more contrast. I let the new sight settle and I peered around, looking for any sign of the village elder.

I saw footprints in the gravelly dirt. Lots of footprints.

I frowned. This must have been one of the destinations the teens had been slipping away to.

Since all the footprints seemed to move in the same direction, I stood and followed, barely conscious of picking my way over the landscape for stealth.

Slowly, the sounds under the crashing waves grew louder and clearer until I could hear voices. I narrowed my eyes as I moved closer to where they were.

The voices were all feminine, higher pitched. They were the sounds I had mistaken for bird cries. I couldn't quite hear what they were saying, so I moved closer, crouching down and placing my feet carefully. I couldn't tell why I felt it necessary to sneak up on them, but I also couldn't shake the feeling.

Before I could get close enough to see who was speaking, a figure appeared in my vision. The yellow over my sight kept me from recognizing the figure at first, but I reached out to test their energy and I knew.

I ducked into a full crouch behind Jeremiah. With one eye on him and my ears straining for the conversation, I let my focus move with the energy of the situation.

Jeremiah leaned forward, listening to the conversation ahead of us. I could hear Catherine's voice, reedy in the gusting winds.

"—don't have to stay here. You can leave...time—"

A richer feminine voice emerged over the crashing waves. "—life's work is here...have as much to lose—"

Catherine's voice came back. "—stop it...won't save us...give us more time—"

A new voice, similar to the unknown one but a little higher pitched, wove through the gusts and crashing waves. "—power...can't control—"

As my eye grew more used to the darkness and the lightning flashes, I spotted several forms on the beach a few yards farther down from Jeremiah. The brief glimpses I caught gave me a focus to read the energies, and I nodded at the confirmation.

The group surrounding Catherine was made up of the researchers. Dr. Roane was no doubt the first of the two voices, and likely the shape closest to Catherine's more short and stocky form. The other scientists were ranged behind the middle-aged woman and, while they lifted hands against the spray of the waves and the shocking bright flashes, their body language was aggressive.

I hadn't been able to discern enough to know exactly what Catherine and the researchers were saying, but, between the words I did catch and their energy, I was sure that Catherine was trying to stop them from doing something bad.

I gasped as the thoughts clicked together suddenly. The research scientists must have the ninth Runespell. They would want to keep the island intact long enough to finish their research, and Dr. Roane's territorial attitude at every meeting reinforced the idea that they were doing something that might not be appreciated by others.

Of course, that meant that whoever held the eighth Runespell was not working with them. None of the scientists had been in the village often enough to account for my irregular bouts of weakness. Or maybe they had someone else do it without knowing.

My thoughts flickered back to my encounter with them and Elizabeth. Dr. Roane had said that they didn't have any of the Runespells, but there was no reason they wouldn't have lied about it.

I cursed myself for a fool for having believed her. Them knowing about the Runespells should have been damning enough to investigate further. Instead, I let their familiar formality be enough to convince me.

And it would have been easy enough for the scientists to embed the Runespell into something, allowing Elizabeth to use it without ever touching it directly. I shuddered, recalling the Healing Rod of Asclepius and my experiences with Zaro.

Anger and fear warred within me for a long moment. When my head cleared, I realized I'd lost the thread of the argument. I checked everyone's positions, relieved to find that no one had moved much while I was distracted.

Cursing myself for my lack of focus, I strained to catch the voices again within the increased winds. I could no longer distinguish words, so I tried to listen for the tone of their speech.

I could tell that the argument was getting more intense, but I still couldn't hear what anyone was saying. How had Catherine gotten involved in this? Had she noticed the strange weather and recognized it as a form of control? With her experience with her grandparent, the alignalghi, she might have seen the signs for what they were.

I considered what my best move would be, hoping for some advantage to come up. As it was, there was a stalemate that didn't help me, but at least it kept everyone in place for the moment. Unfortunately, the storm was a timer that was running out on the impasse.

My eyes flicked to where Jeremiah crouched only a few feet in front of me. He was going to be the wild card, I knew it. But was he going to be a significant player, or just a potential impediment or victim to watch out for?

Ideally, I could just get him to leave so I would be able to deal with the women from the research station. The goal was to stop them, retrieve the Runespells, and keep Catherine safe in the process. Jeremiah's well-being would have to be a distant fourth priority.

I nodded to myself. If he interfered, I might have to remove him from play myself. It would be complicated, trying to handle the researchers, help Catherine, and not abandon Jeremiah to the storm, but I'd figure out a way, even if I had to send some of the other missionaries and villagers after the man.

I shifted on my feet, moving my weight from side to side in a slinky, swaying motion. The movement gave me the chance to make slight adjustments to my stance, testing the way my balance was supported before I moved.

A cry went up from the scientists, and I squinted into the darkness, trying to see any details that might help. Miraculously, I could see them a little better, as if there was more light.

Several of the women were pointing to the horizon. It took me a moment to realize that they weren't looking into the storm, but across it. With a sinking feeling, I moved my gaze to where they pointed. A groan escaped my throat, swallowed by the sounds of wind and surf.

Veils of heavy clouds cris-crossed the moon as it rose higher in the sky, now tinted an almost unnatural dark red. I wrenched my gaze back to the group. My time was up. Rán was coming.

I gathered myself to move, hoping to catch them by surprise enough to make this a quick and easy win.

Jeremiah jumped up in front of me and raced toward the women. Before I could do more than blink in surprise, one of the women started shrieking in anger and fear.

CHAPTER 29

I leapt forward, coming up on the group carefully. Jeremiah had moved to one side and was brandishing a decent sized pocketknife. He held a suede coat in his hands.

The research team all faced him, anger and fear flowing off of them in waves. One of the women, stripped of her coat, stood frail and shivering in the wind. Several of the others surrounded her protectively. Dr. Roane stood closest to the preacher, her posture aggressive, but she made no move toward him.

I spotted Catherine on the opposite side of the group. I caught her eye when I approached. I waved with my hand, gesturing for her to get away. Her expression changed from fear and concern to determination. She began edging away from the group, obviously trying not to draw the others' attention.

I quickly made her escape easier by calling out loudly. "What is going on here?"

Jeremiah flinched, but never took his eyes off the Dr Roane. Only a few of the women even glanced my way. I was taken aback by the level of focus they had on the preacher. I turned to look closer at him.

"They are witches," Jeremiah cried, gesturing toward the women with his knife. "They manipulate the weather and the sea with their demonic powers! They have familiars, and they can turn into those familiars!"

I frowned. "What?"

Jeremiah looked at me at last. There was a fanatical light in his eyes as he tried to convince me of what he was saying. "They are agents of evil!" He hesitated as if seeing me clearly for the first time. "You won't believe me," he wailed. "You aren't a believer."

I shook my head. "Tell me," I entreated. At the very least, I would keep him busy and possibly distracted. "Tell me what you know. I will... try to believe."

His eyes flicked between me and Dr. Roane for a long moment. One of the women took a small step forward. The preacher flinched and held up the coat, pressing the knife to the soft fuzzy brown material. Something tickled in the back of my mind, but I pushed away the distraction.

Finally, he spoke. "I've been watching them," he said, strain threading his voice. "For years now, I've been coming here trying to save the people of this island from the demons they unknowingly host."

"You aren't here very much," I pointed out. "How do you know you aren't misreading the situation?"

Jeremiah snorted. "I may not be here, but I have people who keep an eye out when I'm gone."

"People like Tommy?" I asked.

He shook his head. "That man is too reclusive. He never mingles with people. That wouldn't help me. They," he gestured at the women with his chin, "would notice him hanging around them."

A thought struck me. "Stephen spied on them for you?"

Jeremiah's face broke into a grin. "It was perfect. He'd been humping supplies for them for a while before I asked him. He thought there was something weird, but he didn't know what to do about it." He shook the coat in his hand. "He figured out some of it though. These women sold their souls for power and these fancy coats symbolize that. The rest we learned through his niece."

"Stephen's niece?" Dr. Roane asked. "Who—?"

I quickly reviewed everything I knew about the various people in the village and their relationships to each other and to the research station. I narrowed my eyes as another thought clicked into place. "Elizabeth? Is she Stephen's niece?"

Jeremiah nodded, his eyes still bright with the passion of a man who thinks he's justified in what he was about to do. I only wondered what he was about to do and if he had stumbled upon the truth that I was seeking as well. "I knew you wouldn't be as suspicious of a young woman, especially one so outspoken about her people as she is. She was perfect for what I needed."

"That little— Damn her!" Dr. Roane spat.

I shook my head, ignoring the woman's outburst. "What did they find out, Jeremiah? What is your evidence?"

The preacher looked over at me. I could see the sweat on his brow, even with the chill wind blowing against us. I began to suspect we were going to have to come to some kind of conflict before this situation was resolved.

"Tell me," I pleaded, reaching toward Jeremiah. I kept my movements slow and calming, hoping the supplication would appeal to him. "Tell me what you've learned. Tell me how you know what they did."

I watched his eyes flicker across the faces of all of the researchers before coming back to meet my gaze. "It's the seals," he said, finally. His voice had dropped enough that I had to strain to hear him.

"The seals," I asked. "What about them?"

"I had to find a way to keep them from using their animal powers," he cried. The hand holding his knife shook, and I realized he'd wrapped a large silver and black rosary around his fingers. It struck me as odd, considering his previous dismissal of the religious token.

"Their animal powers," I mumbled. "You stop them from using... animal powers?" I felt the blood drain from my face, and I glanced over at Dr. Roane. "Are you... berserkers?"

The woman frowned. "No, we are not. We aren't witches either, or associated with what you call demons," she said, directing her final words at Jeremiah. She turned back to me. "At least not demons in the sense that Christians believe."

I shook my head, trying to place all of the information in a pattern that made sense.

"You are!" Jeremiah cried. "Your power comes from the seals and is stored in these devil-spawned coats!" He brandished the suede in his hand and moved the knife next to the hide.

"No!" The coatless woman lunged forward, held back only by the women around her. I could hear the soothing, sympathetic sounds of their words almost as clearly as I could read the fear and stress in their energy.

I looked back at Jeremiah. Sweat soaked his hair at the temples and I could see where his shirt darkened with the dampness at his neck. His eyes shone in the darkness as he clung to the power he held over the women. He knew something about them, and that it had to do with the coats.

The coats, not the Runespells? The thought tendril wove into my consciousness. I suddenly realized I'd been making a lot of assumptions that needed to be revisited.

I'd believed that the research team had the ninth Runespell. I'd also assumed, with the way the preacher and the women were behaving, that he held the eighth. But those were assumptions. What would the explanation be if one or both of those assumptions were wrong?

My eyes fell on the coat in Jeremiah's hand. My gaze flickered to the group of women. They were behaving as though the preacher held one of them hostage, staying back and placating him as much as they could given how the spikes in their energy showed their anger and distress. And they were very angry and very distressed.

Over a coat?

It was a nice coat. Each of them was a brown furry suede that fit each woman as though made just for her. The coats hung down to just below the hip but hung open.

I peered closer at them and could see no closures. There were no buttons, zippers, snaps or anything else to hold the garments closed against the weather. It was an odd choice for them, given how warm and heavy they would be.

I noticed the women closest to the water had some spray from the waves beaded on the brown fur. It would have to be treated to be water-resistant. Unless it was a natural feature of the material.

I felt my gut churn as the facts fell into place. I turned the result around in my mind, looking for holes before I let myself fully acknowledge it. When it passed inspection and I felt the truth of it, I turned to Dr. Roane.

"You're selkie!"

CHAPTER 30

Dr. Roane nodded, her eyes staying on Jeremiah. "We are," she affirmed quietly.

"See!" the preacher crowed. "She admits she is a demonic creature!"

I rolled my eyes. "Seriously?" I snapped. "Selkie are fae, not demons. Not even daemons, strictly speaking."

Jeremiah's face fell into a scowl. "What— What do you mean?"

I sighed. "These women are no more evil than pixies or brownies."

"Brownies?" The confusion on the man's face was nearly enough to set me laughing.

"You know, like the elves and the shoemaker? Gnomes? Dewdrop pixies?"

"Wh— What? No! They can transform—"

"Stop it!" I cried. The sudden rustle of my hair on my neck reminded me of the oncoming storm, and I glanced behind me at the expanse of ocean. The waves had calmed significantly, and the wind had died down while we had been caught up in the drama of the preacher and the selkie's coat.

I turned back to the man and stepped forward. "You are not correct, Jeremiah. I'm sorry." I gestured at the women around us. "They are not demons or witches."

His eyes flickered around the group of women. The fanatical light had faded from them, replaced with doubt.

I stepped forward again, taking advantage of the small leverage I'd managed to gain.

"These women are just rare creatures trying to survive among us," I said. "And aren't all creatures God's creatures? Are you so prideful as to decide that one of his creations is wrong?"

Jeremiah's face twisted as several emotions crossed his features. When he frowned and shook his head, I knew he wouldn't be reached with that logic.

Rather than continue to argue with him when he'd obviously made up his mind, I sprang into action. I quickly adjusted my weight before leaping forward with the berserker agility I had gained from the mountain lion spirit. I landed immediately in front of the preacher and grabbed the knife and his hand together.

A sharp pain shot through my palm, but I ignored it, wrenching my hand around until the man released his weapon. Without even glancing in that direction, I threw the knife in a high arc toward the ocean.

Fear filled Jeremiah's eyes and the predator within me reveled in the scent that floated on the soft breeze. I knew my eyes had to be yellow, given how strong the berserker was on me. If there had been any doubt left in me as to whether the preacher had the eighth Runespell, it was gone now. He'd have surely used it by now.

I let a growl fill my throat, and my hands gripped the seal skin coat in his grasp. "It's time you give this back," I snarled. "You wouldn't want to be labeled a thief." I tugged sharply, pulling the fur from him. I held it out behind me, still staring the preacher down. It was removed from my grasp almost immediately.

Jeremiah stared at me in shock for a moment, then his expression turned to anger. "You are as bad as they are," he spat. "You are a witch!"

I laughed in his face. "Yes, I am," I said. "For nearly 20 years now, and proud of it." I let my expression become deadly serious. "You should be happier about that, given what I must do."

The preacher blanched. "Wh—what do you have to do?"

I reached for the man, fighting nausea about what I was about to do. "I must save the world," I muttered. "And you really need to be okay with that."

I touched his cheek lightly with one finger, pulling at the power of the first Runespell. After a brief hesitation, Jeremiah's eyes rolled back in his head. My eyes shifted to a spot behind him, and I tried not to remember the feeling that the comforting Runespell could give. Even with that effort, I could only hold it for a few seconds before letting the man go.

"Tell me," I muttered into his ear. "Do you have a silver symbol that lets you do your god's will?"

The preacher's eyes rolled in his head and he smacked his lips several times before mumbling his response, "No."

I shook my head and stepped back, letting the man recover from the overwhelming feelings. Finally, he blinked and focused on my face.

"Begone," I snarled. "Lest you feel the anger instead of the seduction of my power."

The preacher shook his head to clear it, then his eyes widened and he let out a wordless cry. He flung himself backward, falling onto his ass. He scrambled through the brush as if I were advancing upon him instead of standing still, watching his panic.

When Jeremiah disappeared into the darkness, I turned to the women behind me. They stood watching me without expression. The woman whose coat I'd recovered was shrugging into the fur.

Dr. Roane stepped toward me. "Thank you," she said. "We owe you a debt."

I considered her words. As fae, her words meant more than just a polite thanks. She was saying that I could actually ask for a fae favor from them. I nodded, thinking that was a nice ace to keep in the hole.

I hesitated another moment, trying to figure out how to word what I needed to ask. "With all due respect," I began, bowing my head in the researchers' direction, "and I will not ask you thrice. You spoke the truth about not having a Runespell, but how did you know about them?"

Dr. Roane smiled. "We take the passing of our knowledge and traditions very seriously," she said. "That includes the times we have crossed paths with the gods and their toys. The Runespells pop up occasionally in the human world, and it never bodes well for us, so we tend to notice such things."

I nodded. "Well, hopefully, I'll get them out of general circulation soon enough."

The selkie exchanged glances and the women, one by one, strode into the breaking waves. After the waves reached their knees, they dropped into the water, popping up with the puppy-faces of seals after a moment and swimming away.

I watched with fascination, respecting the fact that the fae were honoring me by letting me see them transform. Dr. Roane was the last to leave, and she hesitated another moment before she stepped into the surf.

"You need to talk to your friend," she said to me.

"Friend?"

The doctor nodded. "The one who speaks to the spirits." She dove into the surf.

It was an odd sight, watching a middle-aged woman dive fully clothed into the water. Another moment later, dark, sleek shapes wove over the surface of the water. The seals porpoised quickly out into the dark sea.

I took a deep breath and let the tension I'd been holding go. I'd taken care of Jeremiah and saved the selkie, despite my previous misunderstanding of their situation.

I considered Dr. Roane's final words. "The one who speaks to the spirits." I shook my head. I knew too many people who could speak to spirits, so that wasn't much of an elimination. But who would the selkie know about?

"Nicola?"

I turned to find my mother watching me. "Mom? What are you doing here?"

She looked around the beach. "Jeremiah came running past, ranting about witchcraft and demons, and..." She looked at me. "You."

I sighed. "Oh, well. Jeremiah... he went off the deep end." I caught Mom's look of disbelief before I continued. "He tried to attack the research team. He said they were evil demons who use their coats to turn into seals."

"He attacked...?" She shook her head. "He seemed so nice. But those women..." She trailed off. "He attacked them? You're sure?"

A memory flashed through my mind and I held up my hand, showing the cut on my palm from the preacher's knife. "Yeah, I'm sure."

Her face went pale in the dim light. "Oh. Oh, dear." She seemed lost, as if her world had been shaken. "I-I thought you were overreacting—"

"Mama!" Twin voices rang out in the dark. Two small shapes hurtled toward me in the darkness. A third dark shape followed more slowly.

I caught the girls as they flung themselves at me. "What are you doing here?" I asked, trying to keep the anger out of my voice. "The storm—"

"They wouldn't stay with me once your mom came to find you," Cora said, emerging from the shadows. "It was all I could do to direct them to the right place." She shook her head.

I knew how headstrong my girls could be, so I quickly forgave Cora for not controlling them. I shot a look at my mom, wondering how she was taking the twist. She had her lips pressed together, but I couldn't tell if she was upset with me, Cora, or the girls.

I shook my head. "Well, you found me," I said. "And thank goodness you did. It's past time to get out of this weather."

I glanced up to find Cora and my mom both staring at me.

"What?"

Cora pointed out to the ocean. "Didn't you notice?" Cora said. I followed her gesture, realizing for the first time what it meant that the wind had softened into a breeze. The heavy clouds that had moved in so quickly had faded into a sparse, wispy veil that covered the moon. "The storm is gone. The only sign left of it is the blood moon."

As I took in the cloud reddened orb, I felt the blood drain from my head so fast I got dizzy. I staggered for a moment, trying to fully grasp the situation.

Then my mother asked, "Did you find... what was her name? Catherine?"

CHAPTER 31

Catherine.

I felt horrible. I'd forgotten all about Catherine in the drama of Jeremiah and the selkies. After all, I was only on this beach because I had been concerned for her safety. But then I'd had to save the selkie from the preacher and Catherine had escaped the tense situation.

I frowned. Except that Jeremiah had been spying on the women when I came upon them. The selkie had been arguing with Catherine. I had thought Catherine was telling Dr. Roane not to use the ninth Runespell. Only the selkie weren't in possession of the Runespell.

I replayed what I could remember of their conversation in my mind. The wind and waves had made so much noise that I hadn't been able to hear very clearly.

Now the wind and waves had calmed. And the moon was red. Rán was coming. The Runespell had been used again, I was sure.

Catherine.

I shook my head in denial. "No," I said. "No, Catherine!"

I took off running in the direction the elder had gone. My legs felt weak and I scrambled to keep my footing on the patches of loose gravel and sea spray slicked grasses.

"Catherine!"

I could hear Cora, my mother, and the girls yelling behind me as I ran. I didn't slow down, even when my knees tried to buckle.

"Catherine!" I roared.

Ahead on the beach, a shadow shifted, turning toward me. I raced toward her. My anger faded as soon as I felt it, but the desperation stayed.

If Rán came for the Runespell, with my mother and children on the beach...

I skidded to my knees a few feet away from the elder. She looked down at me with sad eyes, as if she knew what had to happen.

"You are the one who calmed the storms," I croaked, my voice harsh from trying to catch my breath.

She sighed and turned to look out onto the ocean. "It is my duty to my people," she said. "Passed down through my family. We protect this land from the ravages of the waves and wind. We demand that the spirits leave us in peace when they try to take too much. We are alignalghi."

I realized Catherine was holding something in her hands, clasped together at her waist. I craned around to see it more clearly, but the light was too dim. I'd lost the last bit of the berserker that had gotten me through the encounter with Jeremiah.

"Nicola!" my mother cried as the others came up behind me.

"Catherine!" Cora gasped.

I ignored them all. "You have to stop, Catherine," I plead. "The forces you are angering are more powerful than you know. Stop now, and I might be able to save you."

She turned her head to meet my eyes. "Still trying to save us, Taquka'aq arnaq? I told you we cannot be saved."

I pressed my lips together. "You also let me believe you weren't the one using a Runespell to calm the storms."

Catherine shook her head, shifting her hands to reveal a star-shaped bulge on the end of a stick. "Not a Runespell, child." She held it out so I could see it in the ruddy light of the red moon.

It was a rawhide wrapped stick, about 6 inches long. It ended in a stiff rawhide balloon, shaped like a person. The head, arms and legs were splayed out, forming a star, and a tuft of fur decorated the head.

I examined it closely, but I couldn't see any glints of silver. "But I was sure..."

Catherine shook the stick sharply, creating a hollow rattle in the balloon. "We have our own magics," she said. "Older than yours. But you never want to give us that credit."

I frowned. The chances that two items with identical abilities were in the same place, with one of them being hunted by a jötun, as well as by me – it just seemed a little too much to believe.

"It told you how to use it," I said. "When you first picked it up, it literally spoke to you."

Catherine's expression turned to shock. "H-how...? The spirits told me. They help us when we need it."

"Yeah, I know they do," I said. "But, in this case, I don't think it was your spirits."

Her lips pressed together and her features hardened. I knew she was digging in with her belief.

"Learn to carve them, learn to read them, learn to stain them, learn to validate them, learn to summon them, learn to modify them, learn to share them, learn to use them." I spoke firmly, reciting the Runespells chant that I'd heard each time I'd touched one of the Runespells for the first time.

Catherine's eyes widened. I could tell she recognized the words. She'd touched a Runespell.

"Tell me how it happened, Catherine," I said. "I need to know if I'm going to be able to help you with this. It isn't about your culture anymore. It's about the gods themselves getting involved. And you are at the center of it." I leaned forward. "Let me help you."

The elder's shoulders slumped and she let her head hang down for a moment before she spoke. Her words were so soft, I almost missed them.

"My grandfather was alignalghi. The last one in our village. My mother refused to believe in the power he could wield, but I knew Grandfather could summon the spirits to calm the winds. When he knew he was at the end of his life, he began to train me. He showed me the rituals and told me the stories that would guide me. He gave me all of his knowledge, but he left out one thing." She held up the rattle. "This. This was the sacred item he used. I knew that much, of course. But he never gave it to me to practice with. He showed me, over and over, but he never let me touch it."

I struggled to my feet, annoyed with the weakness that still caused my legs to wobble. "What happened then, Catherine? How did you get the rattle?"

She lifted her head and met my gaze. Her eyes shone with tears, the moisture glinting in the low light. "I touched it," she choked out. "He was sleeping, and I could no longer resist the temptation." She looked down at the rattle. "It was so old and powerful. I could always feel the power coming from it, from the spirits it summoned. When my hand brushed along the bulb of the rattle, it was as if time stopped."

"And you heard the words?" I asked. I was desperate to peer out over the ocean, to see if the storm goddess was coming. Instead, I focused my will on the elder, encouraging her to reveal her secrets.

Catherine nodded. "The words flowed over and around me, brought by the spirits themselves. And I knew." She reached out a hand to grip my arm. "I knew how to use it. I knew how to make the spirits do my bidding, in this, at least." She let her hand fall away. "I knew. But then time rushed back in, and Grandfather was dead."

I bit my lip, empathy for the woman washing over me.

The elder turned her head away. "It was my fault. He died because I touched the sacred rattle. The spirits demanded a sacrifice for the knowledge they gave me. I'm sure of that." She raised her chin and stared out at the sea. "That was my first lesson as a full alignalghi – the spirits can be cold, harsh, without compassion."

She turned to look at me. "That's a lesson you, too, have learned."

I nodded. "Yeah. It sucks." I sighed, remembering for a moment before pulling my attention back to the problem at hand. "You understand that your sacred rattle contains the Runespell I'm looking for, the Runespell the storm goddess wants under control?"

Catherine hesitated. "You will destroy the rattle. My grandfather's rattle. The last sacred tool of the alignalghi of this island."

"No!" Cora gasped from behind us.

I glanced back at her. I'd almost forgotten the others had followed me. My mother and the girls stared at me, wide-eyed. Incongruently, my mother had one hand in the pocket of her jacket. I frowned at her.

"You can't do this," Cora said, interrupting my thoughts.

She stepped toward us and I dropped into a defensive crouch on instinct. Immediately, I felt another wave of weakness come over me. My knees buckled and I fell to the ground.

I glared at Cora. "You!" I growled. "You will pay for this!"

CHAPTER 32

Cora stepped back, her eyes widening a moment before she recovered. "What—?"

I struggled to my feet and staggered toward her. She hesitated before lunging forward to catch me as my burst of strength drained out of me.

I clung to her jacket and dragged her down with me, falling to my knees once more. Her expression showed sympathy, and I hoped I could appeal to that sympathy.

"Please," I begged her. "Stop it. I have to do this. Rán is coming. She will kill us all if I don't."

Cora glanced up at Catherine, then back down at me. "Wh-what do you mean? Why do you want to destroy our artifacts? We have so little of our culture left."

I tugged at her lapels. "You won't have anything left if I don't. Rán is not compassionate. She isn't merciful. She will swallow this island into the sea without a second thought if she decides that's what needs to happen." I pulled myself up straighter, desperation giving me strength where the berserker rage could not. "I'm trying to stop that from happening."

Cora stared at me for a long moment. Then her shoulders slumped and she nodded. "Okay, fine. I believe you."

I sighed in relief and waited for my strength to return. When it didn't, I frowned up at her. "You have to help me," I prompted. "You have to let me do this."

Cora frowned. "I'm not stopping you." She wrapped an arm around me, trying to help me stand. "What is going on? Are you hurt?"

I stared at her, fear filling me. I glanced back at Catherine. "Is it you?"

The elder watched us with a resigned expression and shook her head sadly. "I am doing nothing against you or your spirit, Taquka'aq arnaq. I swear."

I watched her face for a moment then nodded. "Fine, then give me the rattle." I held out my hand for the relic.

Despite her words, Catherine hesitated. She caressed the small staff as if saying goodbye. Then, she heaved a sigh and thrust it into my hands.

I shrugged off Cora's attempts to help me up and let myself fall into a sitting position on the rough gravel beach. I ran my hands over the object, both admiring it as a sacred cultural relic and searching for the sigil I knew it must contain.

The handle was a smooth stick or bone wrapped with a ribbon of bleached rawhide. It was so old it had burnished into a golden tan with the dirt and oils of generations of hands. The bulb of the rattle was formed from two star-shaped pieces sewn together and dried so that the rawhide ballooned out, creating a hollow to hold the sound-making pellets inside.

The bulb was loosely shaped like a person spread eagle, but the fur and paint decorating it added character. The paint gave the dual impression of a turtle and a coat over the rattle's torso, while the fur was glued to form a hood around the vague features of the face. There was some kind of smaller bone embedded through the rawhide of one of the rattle person's hands.

I moved my fingers carefully over the fur and across the rawhide, smoothed by years of handling. When I found nothing there, I moved my fingers over the handle, starting at the end farthest from the rattle and going up. I made sure to touch every inch of the stick as I went.

I reached the base of the rattle with a sinking feeling in my stomach. Then I felt something under my fingers that was slightly too smooth and too cool to the touch. And time stopped.

I didn't hold my breath. There was no breath to hold and no time to hold it. My consciousness simply expanded in the space between one heartbeat and the next.

The familiar chant sounded in my mind, identical to what I'd quoted to Catherine. When the rhythm of the words pounded in my head in place of my missing heartbeat, the words changed.

"I have learned the ninth spell: if the winds and the rains and the waves and the deep threaten lives I want to protect, I can whisper for the waves to soften, for the wind to gentle, for the deep to claim none of those lives."

As time restarted, I pulled at the rawhide binding at the base of the rattle. A segment loosened under my clawing fingers, and a silver pendant fell free. I snatched it up and slapped it onto the chain around my neck as quickly as possible. There was no way I was going to risk something taking my hard-won prize away.

I heaved a breath and took a moment to process what the Runespell did. After a moment, I just shook my head. It couldn't have been designed to be more insulting to Rán if that had been the purpose of it. "Dammit," I muttered, scrambling to my feet.

I held out the rattle to Catherine, but she shook her head. "It is time for another to hold it." Her eyes moved to Cora's face.

I nodded and handed it to the young woman. "Here. Take your people's sacred rattle and get out of here." I glanced around. "And get my family out of here, too. Now."

Cora's expression became bewildered. "What? But—?"

I turned my head, peering out into the ocean. Clouds had gathered on the horizon, but it looked wrong. After staring for a moment at the column of darkness where they blocked the stars, I realized the gathering clouds were too bunched together to be natural. I shivered, knowing what that portended.

"She's coming." I ground out the words between clenched teeth. I was trying to keep them from chattering.

"We can't leave you," Cora protested. She glanced up at Catherine, including her in her words.

"My god, Nicola," my mother said, breaking her silent observation. "What is going on? Why are you trying to get rid of us?" She gathered the girls close to her with one arm. "And who is this— this... Rán you keep talking about?"

"She's the Norse goddess of storms," Cora said.

I knew she was trying to help, but I also knew my mother was not going to be having that answer. I opened my mouth to interject, but my mom spoke first.

"Are you kidding?" she cried. "You are shooing us away so you can play pretend about some... false god? And you were about to attack this woman earlier! What is wrong with you?"

"Mom!" I yelled. "This is not a game. Ella and Maria are in danger! You and Cora, too."

"And what about this poor woman?" Mom asked, pointing to Catherine, who was watching the whole interaction dejectedly.

"I-I can't tell you," I choked out. "You have to go before she gets here. You can't see..."

Cora flinched back, staring into my eyes. Horror filled my mother's face.

"Can't see what?" Cora asked.

"Yes, Nicola," my mother added. "What don't you want us to see?"

I snarled, then bent over, gasping for breath. "Dammit!"

Catherine stepped forward, gently placing her hands on my arms, lending me some small support. She looked up at Cora, then glanced over at my mother. "Ran is coming to..." Catherine's gaze flickered down to the girls. "She is going to demand retribution for what I've done."

"Retribution?" Cora asked. "Like... the salmon?"

Catherine nodded. "Not so drawn out, I suspect," she said. "But yes. I have saved many people over the years, and particularly in the last month. She will want that balance restored by taking me."

I shook my head, tears running down my nose as I struggled to hold on to any strength at all. "I'm sorry, Catherine," I said. "I thought I could... do something."

Mom glared at me. "What do you think you could do?" she demanded. "If this... Rán is real, and if she is coming for Catherine, what could you do? You claim she is a god. Do you fight gods now?"

I looked up, standing as straight as I could manage, still gasping for breath. It felt like my diaphragm had lost all ability to pull oxygen into my lungs. Terror filled me, draining the blood from my face. But I had experienced terror before. I had faced death before. I had to keep going.

I stared my mother down, pulling on my will even through my weakness. "Yes, Mom," I said, putting as much force into my words as I could manage. "I do fight gods."

CHAPTER 33

My mother scowled at me. "You can barely stand up," she bit out. "How are you going to fight a god like this?"

I shook my head. "That's the problem, isn't it? I can't."

The look of triumph on her face was too much for me. I could handle the fact that she was firmly Christian. I could deal with her being against mental health treatments. Even her need to interfere with my parenting wasn't much more than an annoyance.

Her desire to see me suffer for not agreeing with her, though. That was intolerable. That was the boundary I couldn't let her cross. Not without a fight.

I gasped and felt a surge of frustration. It wasn't as if I could fight my mother anyways. Every second I was getting weaker.

I almost laughed aloud at that. Given how my mother hated any sign of aggression from me, this was her pipe dream. She must be thrilled that I couldn't fight, or even argue. Whoever had the eighth Runespell was doing exactly what she wanted—

I froze. I blinked slowly, then met my mother's gaze. Her expression was one of satisfaction. My eyes narrowed for a moment, before I could control my reactions.

I dropped my gaze quickly, hoping she hadn't seen. "Maybe you're right," I said. "I don't really know what I'm doing, and I'm not even really sure that I'm on the right path."

Mom nodded and stood up from where she'd been holding the girls close. "How could you? You get so prideful about knowing all this stuff about these... gods, but you don't know who they are."

"I just wanted to prove I could figure it out on my own." I let a whine creep into my voice. "I wanted to be right. Without you. But I don't think I am. It's so chaotic and scary."

She stepped toward me, moving around the girls. "You should have listened to me."

I nodded. "Mom, can you help me? Can you help me figure this out?" My voice came out pleading. I poured all of my fear and anxiety into it. "I can't do it by myself."

"I know," she said. She reached out to embrace me.

I choked on a sob, feeling a sorrow I hadn't expected to have to deal with filling my throat. "Mom!"

I fell into her arms and slumped against her more frail body. Though I should have been stronger than her, I knew I wasn't. My knees buckled and I barely caught myself from falling. My mother held me upright and I let out another sob, one hand clutching her shoulder.

Mom crooned in my ear, telling me how she would take care of everything. Anguish filled my heart, and I slipped my hand into the pocket of her jacket. My fingers brushed the flat metal coin-like item, and time stopped.

•　　　•　　　•

"Thanks for coming over, Mom," I said. "I know you've been busy, but we do like to see you."

My mother smiled at Ella over the table. "How could I not visit my favorite girl?"

Ella giggled as she slid out of her chair. "Can I play with my dolls now?" She pointed at the soft rug in the living room covered with dolls of all sizes. Their limbs were askew more often than not, and an entire department store worth of their clothing had been dumped on one side.

"Yes," I said. "But don't forget to pick up afterward. I don't want to step on someone's head in the middle of the night."

Ella giggled again and ran over to her toys.

I turned back to my mom. She met my eyes for a moment, then stood up, reaching for the dirty plates.

"Mom," I chided her. "I will get those in a minute."

"It'll only take me—"

"Mom!" I frowned at her until she sat down. "Why do you always make excuses to not talk to me? To not just… sit with me?"

"I don't!" she huffed.

I rolled my eyes. "Fine, but it sure feels like it with you jumping up any time we are sitting alone at a table."

"I was just going to grab the dishes." Her voice was patronizingly patient.

"I know," I said. "There's always a good reason." I hesitated. "It feels like there's always a higher priority to you than I am."

This time my mother was the one to roll her eyes. "I am always here to help you," she protested. "Any time you need me to take Ella for a day or a week—"

"That's Ella," I pointed out. "That does help me, but you don't do it to help me, do you? You do it to spend time with Ella."

Mom pressed her lips together. "I try to help you."

I shook my head, giving up. She was never going to understand how she managed to make me feel like a third wheel with my own child. How she managed to make me feel like a nanny for her granddaughter instead of her daughter. "I'm sorry. Just— Never mind."

I ignored her unhappy expression. Instead, I reached for the large manilla envelope my mom had brought with her and laid on the table when she arrived. I glanced at the back and realized she'd never opened it.

"Why didn't you open this? I sent it to you for that reason."

Mom waved her hand in the air. "It didn't seem like something I should have to deal with. And I don't like getting involved in other people's business."

I bit my tongue on my reply. My mother loved to gossip, so that was only true in the most active, technical sense. She wouldn't do anything involving other people's business unless she was specifically asked, but she certainly made sure to know all about it.

Instead of addressing that, I simply opened up the envelope. "This is something I need you to know about," I said, trying to be patient. "It's for Ella."

I pulled out the documents and passed them over for Mom to look at. She scanned through the Will and the Insurance policy with wide eyes.

"W-what is this?"

"It's from Keith, Ella's father," I murmured. "He gave it to me just before he died."

Mom's eyes jumped up to my face. "You were with him when he died?"

I nodded.

"I thought he was shot..."

I nodded again. "Yeah," I croaked out.

My mother inhaled sharply. "You were there?"

I cleared my throat. "They were trying to kill me, and to shut up Keith. They only got him, though."

Mom sat back in her chair and watched me for a long moment. "How close did you get to being killed?"

I shrugged and barked out a wry laugh. "Which time? They tried a couple times. It was... very close." I swallowed down the memories. "Other people died, too."

She leaned forward on her elbows. "God help me, Nicola. How could you put yourself in that kind of situation? You have Ella to think of! What kind of mother are you?"

I closed my eyes and pressed my lips together for a long moment, trying to get my emotions under control. When I could speak again, it came out hoarsely. "I didn't choose this, Mom. It just happened. And I did what I could in the situation I was in." I glanced up at her. "I did save people, too, you know."

"But you shouldn't be putting yourself in any kind of situation like that! Ella..."

"Ella is fine," I snarled. "And she will stay fine. This will not affect her, I promise that."

Mom flinched back. "Well, then." She gestured to the paperwork. "I guess you got a free ride for the rest of your life, so you won't have to worry about it. You can just go off risking your life any time you want."

I snorted. "That would be never. I don't want to risk my life."

"Then why would you?"

"Because I would be just as evil a person if I could stop evil and didn't," I said.

Mom shook her head. "You just have to be special. You always have." She looked over at Ella. "Just remember, I will always be here for Ella." She emphasized the last two words, unaware of the irony that she was reinforcing what I'd been trying to tell her at the beginning of our conversation.

"Yeah," I said. "I know. And thank you for that. I will not let it come to that, though."

She stood up. "I guess if this is how it's going to be, you'd better get your affairs in order, as well." She walked over to say her goodbyes to Ella.

I stared at the paperwork, not seeing it, not hearing her and Ella talking, not noticing her leave. It wasn't until Ella came to ask for a bedtime snack that I inhaled sharply and came back to the present.

CHAPTER 34

"I have learned the eighth spell: when warriors feel the call to fight, when fighters feel anger, when passions turn to violence, I will calm the fury inside them, and turn their strength to impotence and their fervor into languor."

I inhaled sharply and pushed away from my mother. Tears burned in my eyes as I met her shocked gaze. Without a word, without looking away, I held up the Runespell long enough for her to see that I had it, then placed it against the silver chain at my throat, ignoring the burning cold of the crystal next to it.

"You tried to collar me," I growled. "You think I'm creating these situations where my life is in danger. You think it's my fault this is happening."

Mom pressed her lips together with an expression of disappointment. "Of course it is," she snapped after a moment. "This stuff just doesn't happen to people."

"You think I don't know that?" I demanded. "You think for one second I consider this normal?"

"Then why don't you stop putting yourself and those around you at risk?" she cried. "Why don't you just... try to be normal? Why do you have to always be so... so weird?"

I pointed at her. "You are the one who has put all of our lives at risk," I said, my voice getting louder as the wind picked up. "I might have saved everyone, but I couldn't do anything because of what you did. Now we are all in danger."

She frowned at me. "You keep saying that we are in danger. You keep acting like this is a life and death situation. Aside from a storm, what danger is there? I know you've been through a lot recently, but you are overreacting thinking that a little rain and wind are out to get you."

I laughed. "A little wind and rain, huh? I wish it was that simple." I glared at her. "This wind and rain are sent by Rán, the storm goddess of Norse culture. She is coming for vengeance over the use of the Runespell that Catherine had held. And I was sent to ensure the Runespell was collected from the general population. And to determine who should pay for infringing upon Rán's will."

I glanced back at Catherine. The elder was watching the storm roll in. I turned my gaze to Cora. "Take the girls and my mother back to the village now, before she—"

Catherine's voice rose in a frightened, wordless cry behind me. I glanced back at her and wasn't surprised to see she was staring out over the water. With a sinking stomach, I followed her gaze.

The waves roiled a few hundred yards off the water line, spreading along the horizon for only about half a mile. Clouds boiled nauseatingly above the waves, glowing with near-constant flashes of lightning within their depths.

Striding along the surface of the water, the giantess came toward us. Her blue-green skin looked gray in the sparse light of the moon, but I could see the colors more clearly when the lightning highlighted her not-quite-human features. Barely visible behind her was a strange writhing form that I realized was probably the Kraken's tentacles.

"Shit," I bit out. "Time is up."

I turned back to my mother. She was staring in disbelief, frozen in her fear and shock. Cora backed up several steps, shaking her head as if to deny what her eyes saw. Ella and Maria had dropped to the ground and were clutching each other with eyes wide.

I bent to lift the girls up, pulling at the berserker through my anger at my mother's delay in getting them to safety. With a single surge, I set them on their feet and forcibly turned their heads away from the jötun and her monster.

I made eye contact with each of them, making sure I had their attention, then I kissed each of them on the forehead, and gave them a gentle push inland. "Run! As fast as you can!"

I watched to make sure they had started moving, then whirled around to face the sea goddess. She was close enough now that I could see her eyes flashing like the lightning above her.

Out of the corner of my eye, I caught a movement, and I lunged forward as one of the huge tentacles dropped toward the shore. I moved with a berserker's reflexes, shoving Cora and my mother out of the way, before leaping away as the giant limb impacted the gravel beach.

"Stop it, Rán!" I yelled. "You're just being childish! Get your pet under control and we can talk."

Ran turned her head to look me in the eye. "What makes you think I've come to talk?" She raised her hands over her head and the waves behind her rose up as well, towering close to 50 feet in the air.

"You want to know that the Runespell is out of the hands of people who will use them to sabotage your influence. You will talk."

The goddess stared at me for a long moment, then a horrible smile bloomed on her face. "So be it, quest hero. Let us talk."

I glanced from Catherine to Cora to my mother. The three women were staring up at Rán with expressions of shock. Cora and Mom were sprawled on the ground where I'd pushed them, and Catherine was slowly backing away. I hoped all of them would have the sense to get away before Rán's patience ran out.

"You have found the Runespell?" Rán asked.

I swallowed, searching for a way to delay the inevitable. I just needed to stall for time. "You left me half drowned, you know," I said. "I almost didn't make it. What would you have done then?"

The goddess shrugged her seaweed covered shoulders. "I would have done what I'd planned before you offered to do this work. I would have simply destroyed this island."

I snorted. "And how could you have done that, with the Runespell being used to cancel out your storms?"

Ran lifted her arms out slightly, and the tentacles flailing behind her formed a wall of limbs that somehow conveyed a readiness to attack. "I have other options, human."

I shook my head. "That would have been no guarantee that you would find the Runespell," I pointed out. "It might have been carried away with any survivors of your attacks."

"I have other options for that, too."

The waters around Rán's feet suddenly roiled with activity. Shapes lifted from the waves, and I recognized the puppy-faced seals of the selkie. Rán lifted her chin and watched me.

"The selkies?" I asked. "They are not yours to command."

One of the seal faces seemed to melt away, leaving the features of Dr. Roane. She lifted her head out of the water, surrounded by her sisters. "I'm sorry, Nicola," she said, projecting her voice over the sound of the waves. "We have a debt to the jötun. We must pay it in full."

I clenched my jaw. This was not good news, but I couldn't fault the fae creatures. They were bound by their own rules, unlike humans. For us, free will trumped all else, but fae and gods were bound by other aspects first.

I shook my head. "I understand," I called back to her. "Our friendship is not broken over prior obligations." It was the least I could do to reassure her that I would not abuse their debt to me out of vengeance. Not that it would have been a smart choice. The fae didn't take kindly to pettiness in regard to their debts.

I turned my attention back to Rán. "Fine, then. You might have gotten your way. But some part of you didn't want to destroy all the innocent lives. Some part of you still doesn't, or you wouldn't have approached us with the restraint you have shown."

The sea goddess twitched one shoulder, as if to shrug. "I have no desire to overreach." She smiled that beautiful, horrible smile again. It was like the call of the depths – deadly and seductive, a false promise of relief and peace. "I seek balance, not a swinging of the pendulum to the other side."

"That is very... magnanimous of you," I said. "You—"

"Enough of this," the goddess interrupted. "You have not answered my question, so I will ask once more: have you completed your quest? Or shall I return to my previous plans and find the Runespell myself?"

I swallowed hard as the tentacles haloing Rán moved forward. I could hear the gravel scattering behind me as the women no doubt scrambled to get farther away.

I glanced back to find Cora and my mother holding each other for balance as they backpedaled. Catherine moved slowly and carefully away, as well. I wondered if I would have to sacrifice the woman to save the others. I wondered if she would fight me if it came to that.

The expression on her face was part determination, part fear. My stomach sank. I was suddenly sure that the elder would not go voluntarily.

I struggled to keep my thoughts out of my expression as I turned back to Rán. "Fine," I shouted. "I will tell you."

CHAPTER 35

The goddess of sea monsters stepped forward, her delicate feet finding a steady purchase on top of the roiling waves as she advanced. She stopped just a few feet from where the water rushed over the gravel beach. The wave rising up behind her advanced as well, keeping its height but only forming an intimidating backdrop for her form.

I swallowed hard again and tried to speak around the lump in my throat. I knew it was the fear I was feeling. It was expected. After all, no mortal faced the primordial forces of a jötun without fear. But annoyance still threaded through my mind.

"It was not easy to track down the Runespell," I said. "As I was saying before, I did not arrive here in very good shape. I spent valuable time recovering enough to even move around freely."

Ran watched me impassively as I rambled, but I did my best to ignore the pressure that grew in my gut to simply answer her question. I needed to give everyone more time. It was nearly all I could do for them.

"Once I could move around, even a little, I discovered there were so many interests in play on this tiny island. I had to pick apart the concerns of at least three major groups, and all were suspect for the use of the Runespell."

Tentacles wove through the air, and my breath caught in my throat. But they did not make any moves toward the individuals on the shore. I heaved a sigh, deciding the Kraken was just there for intimidation, for now.

"It took me days to gain enough information and leverage to even begin to narrow down my search. And each time I thought I had, another suspect emerged—"

"I am aware of the complications of human culture," Rán said, making a cutting gesture with one hand. "However, you are still not answering my question."

I opened my mouth to continue with my rambling explanation, but Rán had apparently reached the end of her patience with me.

"You will answer now, or I will take action. And you will not like it." The goddess's voice was as cold as the Bering seawater at her feet. A puff of steam escaped her lips as she spoke, and I realized her anger was literally dropping the temperature around her. It reminded me of the icy crystal at my throat.

I nodded. "I found it. I found the Runespell and it now sits at my throat with the others I've collected. You can take back your stone." I pulled the collection of pendants out of my shirt collar. "I have done what you asked."

Ran reached toward me, somehow stretching across the distance between us. She lightly touched the burning cold spot on my chest. The cold flashed throughout my body for an instant, then was gone.

I gasped and blinked with shock. When the goddess's face came back into focus, she was simply watching me with an impassive expression. There was no sign that she had ever moved, and I clutched at the chain, mentally counting the pendants I found there. I tallied ten small hard shapes, all with the flat, smooth metallic feel of the Runespells. No roundish crystal was among them.

"Great," I said. "Now you can rest easy. No more problems, no more need to interfere—"

"You've done only part of what I asked," Rán said. "You have collected the Runespell, and I will hold you to only using it when the need is great."

I nodded my agreement. "As it should be, so it will be."

"But the insult against me has been great, and I require restitution," she finished.

I shook my head in denial. "That isn't necessary," I said. "The use of the Runespell was not intended to be an insult to you. It was borne of desperation and a desire to protect, not a need to control."

Ran's expression never changed as she watched me argue my case. When she spoke, it was with the cold inevitability of a glacier. "I allowed that I might be swayed to forgive a child, one not capable of truly grasping what they were doing. Ignorance of my nature and existence, however, are not acceptable conditions for such mercy."

I heaved a sigh and lifted my chin. "Well, the only one you know for sure has touched the Runespell is me," I said, trying to keep my voice steady. "And I cannot, in good conscious, give you any other for your vengeance."

"Nicola, no!"

"You can't do this!"

"Don't!"

The trio of voices behind me pulled at my attention, but I waved them off. "I will not send someone to suffer when they don't deserve it."

"You do not have the right nor the power to decide who deserves it." Rán crossed her slender arms across her chest. "And I will not give you that power."

I shook my head. "Well, I won't tell you who you are looking for, so it sucks to be you."

Ran's lips flashed into a smile. "That isn't necessary." She waved a hand and I dropped into a ready crouch.

"Nicola, think of your daughters," my mother cried. "Don't sacrifice yourself!"

I frowned, not taking my eyes off the storm goddess. "This is what I do. This is who I am."

I pulled hard at the anger I felt about Rán's demand. I wallowed in the unfairness of the situation, knowing that someone was going to die to salve the ego of this monster who ruled the sea storms.

My sight flooded with yellow, tinged red around the edges. The strength of the mountain lion filled my limbs fully and I reveled in it. The shapes around me stood out in sharp relief with the cat vision.

My ears twitched searching out sounds within the pulsing white noise of the waves and the gusting wind. Gravel shifted and crunched under my feet, and I heard similar sounds behind me from the women still backing away.

A wave of annoyance at how slow they were fed into the berserker. My lips curled into a silent snarl. "Whatever you have in store for me," I growled at Rán. "I am ready for you."

The goddess smiled icily. "Are you?"

I shivered at her expression, but I glared at her. I spread my arms slightly, curving my fingers to take advantage of the sharp, hardened claws my fingernails had become since I first embraced the berserker. "Yes, I am—"

Catherine cried out behind me, followed by Cora's voice rising up.

"No! Let her go!"

I spun around ready to fight off tentacles or whatever sea beast Rán might have sent ashore. My breath caught at the sight of three women in fur coats grasping Catherine by the arms.

"What are you doing? Dr. Roane?" Catherine's tremulous voice rose as the women pulled at her.

The doctor spoke calmly, despite the effort she was making. "We have a debt to fulfill, Catherine. And you owe the Lady of Storms."

I swallowed, not sure what to do. Technically, the selkie were in the right. Catherine was the guilty party, and they apparently were only clearing a debt to Rán by revealing her. On the other hand, Rán would undoubtably kill Catherine for her actions, and Catherine didn't deserve that. I couldn't let the selkie turn Catherine over to the goddess, but I shouldn't stop them either.

I took a deep breath and closed my eyes, letting my gut tell me what to do. Catherine cried out in pain and my eyes snapped open. I leapt forward without another thought.

Snarling, I slashed my claws at one of the women. She jumped back with a startled yelp and wailed when my nails scratched along her coat. The other two selkie dropped their holds on Catherine's arms, letting the elder fall to the ground. They rushed to defend their sister.

I feinted to the left, then shoulder-rolled to the right, placing myself in a low crouch between the selkies and the Yup'ik elder.

"You can't do this!" I snarled. "I won't stand for it."

The women glanced seaward and nodded. Dr. Roane turned back to me. "Very well," she said. "But the responsible party has been revealed. You've lost the advantage."

She joined her sisters running into the waves for a few strides before they dove into the water. A moment later, more seal faces appeared behind Rán. They watched for another long moment, then disappeared under the surface one by one.

I turned to Rán. Her face had shifted into an expression of satisfaction.

"So this is the one," she said. "I will take her now."

CHAPTER 36

"No!" Cora cried.

"I can't let you do this," I growled, but my words faded as I watched one of the flailing tentacles advance.

"You may fight me," Rán said. "But I will destroy you all if necessary."

"Dear God protect us!" my mother cried out.

I glanced behind me. Frustration flooded through me when I saw that neither Cora nor my mother had retreated farther than the sparse scrub line several yards from the waterline.

"Is there something confusing about 'Run!'?" I growled, half to myself.

Both of them were staring up at the sky above the storm goddess's head. The tentacle had come close enough for the unaided human eyes to see it as well.

My eyes darted around, searching for some advantage I might have. There was nothing to stop Rán and her monster except for me, my berserker, and the Runespells I had around my neck.

A quick mental review of those pendants gave me a flash of inspiration. I dug into my pocket pulling out the lighter I'd used to light fires at the celebration what seemed like years ago. Without hesitation, I flicked the lighter and pulled on the seventh Runespell with my will.

Flames leapt from the lighter and formed a semi-circle around me and Catherine. The descending tentacle recoiled from the fire and a deep bass roar sounded from across the waves. Keeping my concentration centered on the flaming barrier, I reached out to help Catherine to her feet.

"You need to run," I said. "Take everyone with you. You have to get out of here."

"Nicola, stop." Catherine's voice was calm, at odds with her situation. "Tell me the truth, Taquka'aq arnaq. Can you stop her?"

I pressed my lips together. "I can try."

"But can you stop her? Do you stand a chance? Do we stand a chance?"

I stared at the tentacles, willing the flames to keep circling. After a moment, I shook my head. "No. Not really."

I felt her hand on my arm. "Then stop trying to save me. The battle is already lost."

I flinched, remembering our earlier conversation. We had spoken of the same problem: my efforts to save a people that couldn't be saved. "I can't just let you—" I choked on the words.

"I'm sorry, Nicola, but you have to." She stepped forward so I could see her with my peripheral vision. "This is how we make all of this right."

"It isn't fair!"

Catherine stood silent for a moment. The tentacle advanced again but recoiled when I made the flames flare up.

"Do you remember what I said about the spirits?" the elder asked finally.

I shrugged. "A bit."

"Nature isn't pretty. Nature isn't fair. The sprits sometimes take too much. They sometimes take the wrong person, or for the wrong reasons. But that's our perspective. That's our human sense of fair and right. Not theirs."

I swallowed. My eyes burned with tears I couldn't shed.

"Sometimes, we just get the short end," she said. "We are a part of something so much bigger, and that needs to be balanced."

"Balanced," I murmured. "Moderation. The stick instead of the carrot." I shook my head. "She needs to use her stick, even if it's unfair to you. She needs to make the point to the rest of us."

Catherine stayed silent, watching me.

I sighed and turned my head to look at her. "Alright. But I let you do this under protest." I hesitated. "My friend."

The elder nodded and pulled me in for a hug. I took another shaky breath and let the flames die out in the wind. Catherine stepped forward.

"No!"

Someone rushed up behind Catherine, grabbing her and pulling her back. It took me a moment to realize it was Cora.

"Stop it!" I cried. "You can't interfere!"

I grabbed her arm and pulled her from the older woman. Cora turned and slapped me across the face. The impact stung, and the yellow in my vision flared red for an instant. I wrestled my emotions under control and turned back to the two Yup'ik women.

Cora had a grasp on Catherine's arm once again. Before I could act, a flash of movement from the corner of my eye caught my attention. I sprang forward, knocking both women down and out of the way of the cable-like tentacle that crashed down where we'd stood.

The thud of the impact shook my insides, and I scrambled up, looking for the next attack. Lightning lit up the sky, but no boneless limbs showed against the flashing clouds.

Catherine cried out and I turned back to the two on the ground. Cora was pinning the elder down, crying "you can't go" over and over. I gritted my teeth against what I had to do.

I rushed over and grabbed Cora around the waist, heaving her up and away from the elder. To all of our shock, her kicking feet caught the older woman at the temple and she fell to the ground, her eyes fluttering.

I threw the young woman aside. She scrambled to her feet and I took a defensive stance between her and Catherine.

"I didn't mean to," she cried.

"I know. But you have to go, or you'll be in danger, too."

"But Catherine—"

"I got her." I put all the reassurance I could into my voice. "Get inland so I don't have to worry about you, too."

"She was going to let..." Cora trailed off, her eyes flickering over to the sea. The storm goddess stood on the surface of the ocean with a stony expression, watching us.

"I know," I said. "But she's half-conscious now. I'll take care of her. Get clear." I waved her off and turned to the elder.

Catherine's eyes fluttered as I reached around her to pull her up into my arms. I paused at the sight of the ring on her finger, a plain gold band. I wondered that we had never discussed any husband or children she might have had. I shook my head in dismay. So many conversations I would never have with last alignalghi.

"You thought you would just walk up to Rán, huh?" I muttered. "Save me from having to actively do this shit. Best laid plans of heroes and alignalghi, am I right?"

I stood up, holding Catherine in a bridal carry. With the strength of the berserker, fed with my anger at how the situation had played out, she was as easy to carry as a toddler.

I was facing inland, and I looked for Cora and my mother. They stood surrounding the smaller forms of Ella and Maria. All four of them had turned to watch me.

"Well, fuck," I said. "Nothing like an audience for the hard stuff."

I turned and ran toward the waterline. The high-pitched screams behind me told me that the witnesses had realized what I was doing.

Tears sprang up in my eyes, turning my vision watery as I hit the waves, sloshing through the surf. I pulled at the first Runespell with my will, hoping that the comfort would help Catherine with what was coming.

I waded out until the water covered me to the waist. The icy water numbed my legs, but I ignored it. I looked up at the figure hovering on top of the waves before me.

"Ran, Jötun, storm goddess, mistress of monsters, bringer of death at sea," I cried. "Take your sacrifice!"

One of the waves rose higher than the others, then broke to reveal a tentacle. The limb wrapped around the woman in my arms and pulled her away, dragging her under the waves. The salt water splashed onto my cut palm and I let the burn wash over me, reveling in the pain.

"She has gold," I pointed out. "A ring. Once you are done with her, release her spirit to the afterlife of her people. She didn't mean to insult you, but she was willing to accept your price. I am asking you to honor her actions by making it fast and releasing her soul when you have taken the life you demanded."

Ran stared down at me for a long moment, then nodded once. "I swear it will be so, but the flesh, I will keep."

I swallowed hard, knowing that she meant to feed her pet. I nodded agreement. I was getting really tired of jötun goddesses and their feeding creatures with people's bodies. Logically, it didn't matter what happened to the physical form once it had died, but it still sat wrong in my mind.

"Then the debt is cleared?" I asked. "For me and for the island?"

Ran nodded.

"And for the selkies?"

Another nod.

"And my quest obligation to you is done?"

"Yes, mortal hero." She hesitated. "I acknowledge the honor of your morals, though they have conflicted with my goals over much."

Without another word, she turned and strode out into the storm. Once she was out of sight of even my enhanced vision, the storm cleared, and the waters were empty of her, the selkie, and the tentacles of the Kraken.

I turned and waded back to shore, my cold-numbed legs struggling against the water. My soaked shoes finally crunched on the dry gravel above the waterline and I staggered to a halt.

"What the hell did you do?"

CHAPTER 37

I raised my head to face the group on the beach. They all had expressions of horror and disbelief on their faces. Cora was crying, and Ella kept wiping her hand across her eyes. My mother stared at me as if she were looking at one of Rán's sea monsters, and I supposed she wasn't too far off on that.

I glanced down to see what Maria's face told me. Her eyes stared up at me without emotion. My heart broke as I read the disappointment and resignation in her eyes.

"I told you to go," I said.

Mom nodded. "So, you wouldn't have to live with us knowing what you did, and what kind of... person" - she spat the word at me like an insult – "you really are."

I sighed. "Partially, yeah. It's gonna be hell living with the knowledge myself. Now I get to deal with you knowing, too. And judging me."

Cora screamed wordlessly and lunged at me. Her fist connected with my jaw and my head jerked back from the impact.

I brought my gaze back to her, clenching my fists at my side. The berserker in me wanted to fight back, to get it out, but Cora needed it more. So I simply looked at her, my eyes burning with unshed tears.

The young woman watched me for a moment, as if she expected me to react somehow. It was what I would expect. When I didn't come at her, she cried out again and hit me with both fists, one after the other.

Again, I simply brought my head back around to face her. My lip burned and I could feel a swelling on it with my tongue.

After another pause, Cora went all out. She hit me with both fists in the chest and knocked the breath out of me. I pulled on the berserker rage then, but only to stay on my feet, though bent at the waist.

She brought her fists down on my back like a pair of hammers, pummeling me over and over. I staggered under the blows, losing count of how many she delivered.

The sound of my blood rushing filled my ears, blocking out the sound of her strangled screams. I grit my teeth and let her hit me.

She finally ran out of steam and ended with a flimsy kick at my face that missed but landed her on her ass. I stood up, wincing at the bruises that were already forming. I took a step over to her and held out my injured hand to help her up.

She screamed at me and tried to throw gravel in my face, but her aim was off and her arm weak. "Leave me alone!"

I sighed, waiting for another moment before I nodded and turned back to my daughters and my mother. I took a step toward them, reaching out to them, but the girls flinched back. My mother stepped in front of them as if she needed to protect them from me.

I sighed again. "Fine," I said. "We'll talk later."

Mom snorted in disgust – or was it disbelief. In the greatest of ironies, she finally did what I'd asked and took the girls, leading them up the beach and toward the village.

"Day late, dollar short," I muttered.

I stood watching them leave, then turned to where Cora was getting to her feet. I made no move to help her, nor did I try to talk to her again. I simply waited impassively until she stalked past me with only a glare, then I followed.

Cora walked fast enough that she overtook Mom and the girls just before they reached the village. I watched each of them go into their respective shelters, then found a dryish spot next to the community center and sat, waiting for dawn.

I must have dozed off because the next thing I knew, the sky was a slightly lighter shade of black with a shot of blue along the eastern horizon. Amazingly, the sea was so calm it was nearly flat as a table.

I looked for what might have awoken me, and found Cora and Mary walking toward me. I considered getting to my feet, but I was taller than both women and I didn't want to appear to be trying to intimidate them.

Instead, I sat with my head laying against the wall of the building. The lack of energy wasn't acting either. I felt completely worn out and sore everywhere. My hand throbbed in rhythm to my heartbeat.

Mary was using her walking cane and planted the heavy stick right in front of me. I turned my eyes to look at her under my lashes.

"I wouldn't have thought you would be a murderer," Mary said, after several minutes. "I'm usually pretty good at judging people. So it makes me curious. Why? Just... why?"

I lifted my head from the wall and looked down at where my fingernails played with the seam on my jeans. "It's complicated," I warned.

When the older woman nodded her understanding, I shifted to face her better. "When I was in the water during the shipwreck, I was pulled down into an undersea cave. There I met the Norse goddess of sea storms." I paused a moment, trying to decide what else to include in my summary. "She had come to the conclusion that someone was using one of these magical pendants to calm her storms, and she wanted that person to pay for the insult of taking away her power. I told her I would help but that I couldn't promise her the life of whoever it was. She agreed and spat me out a few miles offshore."

I took a deep breath and eyed the two women, trying to gage how much I'd just confused them. They exchanged glances and frowned at me, but Mary gestured for me to continue.

"You probably noticed that I was asking a lot of weird questions about who might benefit from stopping the storms."

Cora nodded at that.

"I didn't get very far with that," I admitted. "There were just too many people who fit that. It wasn't until tonight that I finally got some answers."

I heaved a sigh and shook my head. "I followed Catherine to make sure she got to safety before the storm hit. I found her arguing with Dr. Roane, instead. Jeremiah was hiding behind some brush, watching them." I shrugged off the memory. "Turns out Jeremiah thought the scientists were witches. Turns out they were actually selkie – seal women, a type of fae."

"Oh," Cora said. "That's why they..."

"They helped Rán," I finished for her. "They owed her a debt. They didn't offer details." I hesitated, trying to remember where I'd left off. "So the storm was calmed, but the two big suspects weren't the ones doing it. I found Catherine. That's around when my mom, the girls and Cora showed up. Catherine admitted she had been using the rattle to talk the spirits into calming the seas. I found the magic pendent embedded in the wrapping of the handle. "

Cora cleared her throat and looked away when Mary turned to her. The older woman waited until Cora nodded before focusing her gaze back at me.

"I did try to get all of you to leave," I said. "I told you to go several times."

Cora nodded reluctantly.

"I knew she was coming," I continued. "I knew Rán would be there soon, and I figured if I could show her that I'd found the pendent, I might be able to talk her out of her vengeance, but with all of you in the line of fire, I didn't have the leverage I needed to do that."

I held up my hand when Cora opened her mouth to protest. "I know you didn't know what was going on. I don't blame you. I'm just telling you why things went the way they did."

I shifted, noticing the uncomfortable pressure from sitting still too long. "You pretty much saw what happened with my attempted negotiation. It didn't work. I just couldn't get the upper hand. What you probably didn't see, or hear, rather, was me trying to talk Catherine into running for it." I shook my head. "She said it wasn't fair, but it was like the salmon spirits taking too much. It was the price, and it had to be paid."

I looked up, meeting Cora's eyes. "You caught the end of it, though. That's why you tried to stop her from giving herself to Rán. When Catherine was knocked out, I had a choice and knowledge." I held up a finger. "I knew Catherine would rather sacrifice herself then endanger the entire island with Rán's anger." I lifted a second finger. "I knew Rán was out of patience. So I took Catherine to Rán."

Cora covered her mouth with both hands at the memory. Then she blurted out, "She must have been terrified, being so out of it when that creature took her."

I shook my head and lifted the chain of Runespells from my neck. I picked out the first and held it up. "This one gives people comfort. It is a dangerous one, because it overcomes all other feelings, even fear. It can make a person ignore dangers and bad situations. That's how strong it is." I shuddered at the memories of my own experiences with the Runespell.

"You used it on Catherine?" Mary asked. "You gave her comfort instead of fear for her final moments?"

I nodded, my throat closed with guilt and pain.

"That's more than any person can expect at their time of passing," the older woman continued.

I looked up to meet her gaze with eyes burning again with unshed tears.

Mary offered me a small smile. "I think you did your best to honor our alignalghi, to respect the wishes of my friend." She hesitated, then her expression fell. "In doing so, you took on the guilt of the act, didn't you?"

I shrugged.

"Wait," Cora said. "Let me get this straight. You fought all of us to do what Catherine agreed to. And when she couldn't do it herself, you did it for her. You committed a sin and a crime to respect her wishes and protect the rest of us?"

I shrugged again.

Cora squatted down in front of me. "You knew we'd blame you. But you did it anyway."

I tried to give her a weak smile, but my lips were trembling. "It's kinda my thing."

Cora stood and heaved a sigh. After a long moment of staring at me, she held out her hand to me. "Come on," she said. "Let's get you cleaned up and fed. You'll probably even have time for a nap before the coast guard arrives."

Too tired to protest, I took her hand.

CHAPTER 38

I stood in front of the coast guard captain, waiting for the heavy hand of the law to land on me. There were enough people willing to tell him how I'd carried an old woman into the ocean to die. I wasn't going to delude myself into thinking that would just be dropped.

But the man ignored me, just as he ignored everyone else. Instead, he watched as his crew asked all of us for our names and what, if any, possessions we might have.

I blinked in surprise and glanced around, confused. I caught sight of Cora and Mary standing nearby. Cora was speaking to one of the coast guard officers with animated gestures. Mary met my gaze and nodded slightly.

The officer touched his hat to Cora and Mary, then made a beeline for me. "Nicola Crandall?" he asked. "I need to confirm a report made for the accidental drowning of Catherine" he consulted his notes "ah, Tudlik."

My eyes flickered over to Cora and Mary. I nodded as the man went through the entirely plausible but mostly fictional account of Catherine's death, being swept into the sea by an unusually large wave while performing a traditional ritual.

The man finished up just as the last of the shipwreck survivors were done being processed. We were herded onto the ship and I felt a sharp pang at being unable to draw out my goodbyes to Cora and Mary, and the few others I'd been mostly friendly with.

The ride back to the mainland was rough, fast and lonely. My mom and the girls actively avoided me. After a few attempts, I decided to give them the space they seemed to want. I wondered how long it would take to mend the rift that had sprung up so firmly between me and my family.

The coast guard set up our flights home, and I somehow ended up on the other side of the plane from Mom Ella and Maria. I fought my nerves the whole way, but I tried to let it be.

When we arrived at the Indianapolis airport, I impatiently waited for my turn to disembark. When I hurried through security and rushed to where we'd left the cars nearly a month ago, Mom's little blue sedan was already gone.

I heaved a sigh and began the long drive home. Since I didn't have a landline and my cell had been destroyed by the saltwater dunking, I had to wait until I got on my laptop to use an online calling app. I tried my mom, but she didn't have a cell or landline either, for the same reasons. It was late enough that I just decided to go over the next day.

Instead, I called up Joseph. He didn't answer, so I left a rambling voicemail for him, and asked him to message me on one of the platforms I knew we both used. I tried to get some sleep, but I was too worried about how much was unresolved.

In the morning, I hesitated to head over to Mom's right away, afraid I'd get there too early and annoy them unnecessarily. I finally drove over just before lunch, thinking I'd offer to treat Mom before taking the girls home.

There were two strange young women sitting in the living room talking to Mom and the girls when I walked in. All five of them looked at me as I entered.

"Um, hi," I said. "Glad to see you guys made it home okay, but it would have been nice to get a message..." I let the words trail off. The expressions were not at all happy or welcoming. "What's going on?"

"Ms. Crandall," the blonde stranger said, standing and holding out her hand to shake. "I'm Kimmi Stanton with Child Protective Services."

I blinked. "What happened? Girls?"

"Ms. Crandall," Kimmi interrupted. "We are here due to a report against you."

"Me?" I asked. Her words sunk in and I felt dizzy with the shock. "What-?"

"Apparently, there was a death that the girls witnessed?" Kimmi prompted. "Your mother is worried that being around you may cause additional trauma to them."

"That wasn't my fault," I muttered. "I told them to leave. It was dangerous."

Kimmi stared at me without expression. I searched her face for any sympathy or understanding, but she and her partner seemed doubtful of my words.

"You don't believe me?" I said. "There's a report from the coast guard..."

"Look, we are just trying to do what is best for your children," Kimmi stated, as if her position was logical. "Isn't that what you want?"

I stared at the woman. If I agreed with her, it would sound like I was admitting something. If I didn't, it would appear that I was aggressive and controlling.

I shook my head, trying not to laugh with hysterics. I raised my head to look at my mother. "You've been trying to brainwash them for months now. Looks like you finally get your way." I turned to Kimmi. "I have nothing to say to you, except you stay away from me and my kids unless and until you have any – and I mean ANY – evidence. Because there is none."

I looked at the girls. "Do you want to come home?"

They looked at each other. Mom and the two CPS workers tried to talk over them, but I ignored their protests. Finally, Ella shook her head and Maria followed suit.

"Very well," I said. "You can stay for a week. Then you are coming home."

"Ms. Crandall, you can't—"

I rounded on Kimmi. "You have nothing to go on except my bitter, bigoted mother telling outlandish tales of how I'm to blame for every natural disaster that touches us. You," I pointed directly at her, "are barking up the wrong tree. Stop trying to break up my family. It's what she wants." I flung my hand at my mom.

"Why would she want that?" Kimmi asked, disbelief dripping from her voice.

"Oh, so she didn't drop the big bombshell on you yet?" I laughed. "Well, I'm evil, you know. She thinks I have no morals because I don't share her religion. She's prejudiced."

Kimmi frowned and looked back at my mom for a moment. "She... didn't say anything about that."

"Well, that's why I haven't done anything right in years," I said. "She blames me for everything, because she thinks it's my evil selfish nature that puts me in the path of any crappy things that happen. Then she blames me for getting me and the girls therapy to deal with it."

Kimmi frowned again. "You have a therapist? And you got the girls therapy?"

I nodded. "Yeah, not that it means anything to her. She thinks I should just power through any traumas."

Kimmi turned back to my mother. "Is this true? This changes a lot about what you've told us."

I broke in. "I get that some crap happened." I looked at the girls. "One week, then it's back to normal. No arguments."

I turned on my heel and left my mother to deal with the heaping pile of BS she'd started. I fumed the whole way home, going over and over what had happened throughout what had been meant to be a relaxing vacation.

I turned into the driveway and jerked the key to shut off the engine. I stared at the house I shared with the girls, standing big and empty next to the imposing height of the forest.

With a sob, I dropped my face into my hands, crying out every insult, choice, loss and consequence. It took hours.

The End

ABOUT THE AUTHOR

Author Sarah Buhrman has been writing for more than 25 years, starting with poetry before moving on to non-fiction and fiction. She lives in the US with two monsters (the kids), an ogre (the hubby), and whatever drama-llama is coming to visit this week. Sarah is the author of *The Runespell Series* and has short stories in several anthologies. She also has a blog via Patreon and makes funny videos about writing on her vlog, Practically Writing.

NOTE FROM THE AUTHOR

Word-of-mouth is crucial for any author to succeed. If you enjoyed *Blood of the Moon*, please leave a review online—anywhere you are able. Even if it's just a sentence or two. It would make all the difference and would be very much appreciated.

Thanks!
Sarah Buhrman

We hope you enjoyed reading this title from:

BLACK ROSE
writing™

www.blackrosewriting.com

Subscribe to our mailing list – *The Rosevine* – and receive **FREE** books, daily deals, and stay current with news about upcoming releases and our hottest authors.
Scan the QR code below to sign up.

Already a subscriber? Please accept a sincere thank you for being a fan of Black Rose Writing authors.

View other Black Rose Writing titles at
www.blackrosewriting.com/books and use promo code
PRINT to receive a **20% discount** when purchasing..